En
Le
Li

# FIRST DEAD BODY

# FIRST DEAD BODY

*Tony R. Cox*

THE CHOIR PRESS

First published in the United Kingdom in 2014 by
The Choir Press

ISBN 978-1-909300-55-2

Many thanks to Stewart Bint, who planted the seed of the idea; Kate Drew and Gerry Kreibich for their encouragement and constructive comments; and Fiona Thornton and Tony Moss for clear and incisive editing. Thanks also to ex-newspaper colleagues everywhere.

# 1

---

SIMON Jardine was cold, wet and miserable. He'd walked to the office in freezing drizzle from his Burton Road flat and was nursing a well-earned hangover. He loved this job as a newspaper reporter, he'd spent months trying to get it, but now all he wanted to do was nurse a sweet, milky coffee or, better still, swing round the lamp post at the back door and pour himself into the Exchange for a hair of the dog.

"Oy, you." Norman on Newsdesk was not good at first names – well, those of the juniors he couldn't remember. "Go see Dave Green. He's got a job for you!"

In his very late thirties, Dave was a hero to all young reporters. He was the chief crime reporter, and looked and acted the part magnificently. From the neck down he looked a little like a poor man's Columbo, or maybe it was the expression that set it off. Black-rimmed glasses perched on a nearly straight, not too fat, rosy nose, on a face that was topped with slicked-back, just greasy hair. It was clear that Dave washed it at least once a week, probably on a Friday so that the just-washed look had gone by first thing Monday morning. He was five foot seven or eight tall, which made "going to seed" a little difficult as that, in gardening terms, usually meant a tall flowering for a short time and then knobbly bits waving in the wind like overgrown parsnips, if they had not been roots, until they died off. Dave's nobbly bits were all under control: arms and torso wrapped in a near see-through, thin-striped, nylon shirt with a collar that had once been boned and firm and was now allowed its freedom, at least on the left, where the wing was heading upwards. Over the shirt was a dark blue blazer with silverish buttons. The arms were slightly too short, and the days when it would have fastened comfortably over his burgeoning middle-aged spread had gone along with the receipt.

Dave was not bandy-legged, but his National Service must have been difficult. With short legs and a lack of enthusiasm in movement of limbs, he would have been the butt of jokes from any soldier with a stripe. He was at his most comfortable sitting down, with his knees pointing at eleven o'clock and one o'clock: not obscene, just relaxed.

Hygiene was not a problem. Dave Green had learned newspaper reporting in his teens and fully understood the need to be in close proximity to people without them reeling back clutching their noses, so he made sure that BO was under control. The same could not be said about his breath, and there was little that copious brushing every morning could do to combat the effect of the beer and whisky chasers each night. Gold Spot spray was the only solution ... and it should have been issued to every reporter along with a pen and notebook.

Dave was an old-school journalist of the very best sort. He was respected by his peers – and even the 'old timers' on the Newsdesk, though they would not readily admit it – and admired by the younger ones. It was not just the glamour of his job, but the fact that almost invariably Dave would write the front page lead at least twice a week. That was not surprising, as crime was usually sensational and juicy, and it appealed to a generation where murder, robbery, burglary, fights and general wrongdoing were just one small step below the sex scandals that seemed to be the prerogative of the national newspapers.

"We've got a body off St Peter's Street, let's go see what's been happening," he said to Simon, grabbing a short, dark mackintosh off the coat stand and shepherding him to the door.

Seeing a dead body was a recognised rite of passage for young reporters. There was a little rush of adrenalin and no small degree of excitement: this would be interesting, a little macabre, but most importantly, Dave would be doing the work and Simon could just observe.

"You look a bit rough for a Monday morning. Good night was it?"

Simon forced a smile. Yes, it had been a good night. He'd spent it in the company of one of the town's rock bands, who'd finished an afternoon practising in the upstairs room at The Mill and then come down to the bar for a chat. Simon was keen to mix his love of rock music with his career in newspapers, and hearing and meeting local bands was a big part of that strategy.

Dave was always keen to help young reporters, especially those he considered showed a spark of talent and a fair bit of enthusiasm. It was also important that they could drink a couple of pints without either becoming stupid or falling over. Being able to take your drink was a vitally important factor in this job.

St Peter's Street was in the shopping heart of the town.

New, post-war concrete and glass atrocities stuck between older, properly designed shop fronts. Boots on the corner was one of the older ones, and it seemed that a couple of intrepid burglars had shinned up a drainpipe on to the roof over the weekend. The police knew there were two because one had obviously panicked and run away, leaving footprints down the alley – two sets of footprints facing one way, and only one the other.

The man lying in the alley was covered by a blanket, but it seemed pointless. He was a long way past needing to be kept warm, and the "cover" meant that every policeman, plus Dave and his junior, could see his legs and feet and, above them, straight into those wide, sightless eyes as he lay on his back with a dark stain under his head.

It had been Dave's idea to "blood" the young reporter, and he'd spoken to the police inspector to set it up.

"It's his first dead one, so can you open up the gruesome bit a little? We don't want him thinking it's all like on the telly do we? He'll be OK: seems sharp enough and he may as well get this bit out of the way before we start sending him to courts and councils and jobs that involve real work," Dave had told him.

Sure enough, it was gruesome, because it was clearly a bloke, but it was also a bit like looking at somebody's dog that had been run over.

Simon did not feel queasy and did not look away, but he knew he was shocked. This really was the first dead body he'd ever seen. It wasn't like in films where the baddies just fell down facing away from the camera, or the goodies always seemed to have a last speech before they closed their eyes. This was a young guy who'd died on his own, on a cold, dark night and whatever he'd said, maybe "Mum" or the name of a girlfriend, no one, apart from his accomplice, had heard.

He snapped out of his morbid reverie. It had been, he decided, fairly impersonal and nothing too horrendous. The dead man had landed in the alley after slipping down the roof, grabbing the gutter and then finding it had rotted away. He must have just kept slipping over the edge before dropping forty feet on to the uneven flagstones. Whatever noise he made, depending on the time of night, would have gone unheard.

"Right, so now you know what a dead 'un looks like. That boy would have had a mother and father, possibly a brother and sister, but he's young so we can probably discount a wife. They'll cart him away and open him up to find out what killed him, but I think we can safely say it was a one-way fall, and from that height he wasn't going to get back up again.

"Looks like he's a wrong 'un, or was, more to the point, but I hope it was a quick death. Would have been horrible if he'd been lying there in pain while he bled to death, unable to move, and his mate just ran off," Dave said, making the whole scene that bit more graphic, imaginary and even more personal. And it was all said within earshot of the inspector, who smiled at Dave's description – one that he had rapidly come to himself and would soon write up in his report.

"Fancy a pint?"

Dave was already walking off towards the Market Place without waiting for a reply. It had only just crept passed 10am and even though Simon was a keen lunchtime drinker, this was a bit early – a cup of tea and a bacon roll would have been better, but Dave was determined to get a pint.

The Dolphin was probably Dave's second home, certainly in terms of hours spent there and the people he regarded as his family. Even at that time of day, there were three men at the bar and two elderly couples sitting at separate tables with half pints of something dark, possibly a thick stout, and two round wine glasses of orange juice. Dave was greeted not so much as an old friend, more as a brother. There were no cries of welcome, just a look up, an acknowledging nod of the head and a "Morning, what you having? Pint?"

The essence of being an efficient newsroom was trust: trust in your staff that they would not be spending every working hour in the pub getting pissed; trust that if they were always in the pub, then it was with the people who provided the news – the police, the councillors, the blabber-mouths of the criminal fraternity. But to get to that exalted position required guile, contacts, or, and more often than not, the "big break"; the exclusive story that would not just make the front page lead, but call for more interviews with more people and a swell of interest that would mean front page stories for the rest of the week.

Dave Green had nearly got there, but not quite. If there was a suspicious death the police might want what they loosely called "public co-operation", and Dave was the first call, either by telephone, or his preferred method, over a pint or two, which they bought, in one of his watering holes. The Dolphin was fine, but a bit too exposed for some stories, and Dave was never one for staying in a single pub. If the draught Bass was up to standard, and it was very rarely not, then any pub within walking distance would do.

Dave had been the man for crime since most of the junior reporters were in short trousers, so he now had two prime roles: using his innate skill and talent to find out what was behind the top crime stories of the day, looking at police strategy, resources, and the personalities behind the news; and as a walking telephone directory and encyclopaedia for every reporter with a "need to know".

This morning there were no policemen wanting Dave's journalistic skills and, faced with the prospect of starting his week with a round of drinks, he found a solution in his young companion.

"Right then. Buy young Fred here a pint, get another one for yourself and one for me and I'll tell you all about this accident on Boots' roof," Dave said as he indicated the older man who'd greeted him, and then eased himself round the cast iron legs of the table on to the bench seat – a good place to see who came in and went out, and even better financially as he would not have to get out to buy the drinks.

"I knew him. Well, I knew his mother. Dave seemed to have lost the aura of confidence and his words were flat. It was as if the body of the young man was more personal and emotional than that of just a failed crook. She had a tough life and young Joe was one of five she had to bring up alone since hubby had been in and out of Nottingham Prison. He simply couldn't keep his hands off other people's property.

"There were rumours that when the boys were young he'd been fiddling with them. I couldn't see it myself: Joe's dad is one of those racist, macho, chauvinist, big-bellied types who love to boast about their manliness and success with women. Moira, his wife and the boys' mother, was best off without him anyway. When she went to the Working Men's Club at Chaddesden, even in summer, she always used to wear a long-sleeved blouse, and she always looked pale. Some say he was knocking her around a bit, and he was certainly the jealous type.

"No, Joe was all right, or so I thought until this morning. He'd had a few scrapes with the law, nothing too serious, but he seemed to be a bright lad. I just didn't see him getting mixed up in burglaries."

What Dave did not say was that he'd first met Moira in court a couple of years ago. She'd seen her husband being sent down for the third time, this time for three years, for hitting some old woman who'd tried to stop him stealing her savings from a pot on the mantelpiece. She'd asked Dave to go easy in his newspaper report. She was worried that if all the details came out she'd lose her little cleaning job at the car dealership and it would affect young Joe.

Dave was an honest, hard-working, scrupulous news man, but there was something about Moira that made him forget to write up the court case. Later that week, he'd just happened to be in Chaddesden one afternoon and thought he might drop in and take Moira out for a coffee. He had the office car, but he parked it a few streets away and walked the rest. Moira was surprised, even a little shocked, to see him there, and her first thought was that something had happened at the kids' school.

"No, no, I just wanted to see how you were and how you were getting on," Dave said. "I thought maybe you'd like me to take you for a coffee or something?"

Moira's face went through a noticeable transition. Fear and shock changed to relief. It started with her mouth, with her lips closing together, her chin lifting slightly, then her eyes brightening a little – and most tellingly she blushed. Dave had been a reader of people since an early age; it was one of the reasons why he was such a good reporter. He'd always followed the old maxim of trying never to ask a question unless you had a pretty good idea of what the answer was going to be.

Dave had had a good look at Moira in court that day and briefly their eyes had met. He knew he was in with a chance, but he also knew that a fling with Moira could be very damaging to his health, considering the criminal past of her husband.

"You'd better come in," Moira said. "I don't want the neighbours seeing us talking. They probably all know now anyway."

Moira quickly decided that going out for a coffee was not such a good idea. She'd lived in Chaddesden for all of her forty years; she was the mother of five kids who were well known in the area, and some for not the right reasons; and her neighbourhood now was stocked full of nosey parkers. So what if someone had seen Dave go in: he could be a policeman couldn't he? Some detectives she'd seen on the telly were as scruffily dressed as Dave Green. And although Dave was a well-known name in Derby, not many knew him by sight.

Dave looked around the sitting room while Moira made coffee. It was an unremarkable house, like so many others built in the mid-Fifties when councils had been in a mad rush to build three-bedroom semis. The format was always the same: front door leading to a hallway with the stairs on the right, lounge on the left, then down the hall to the kitchen on the right and the dining room on the left. It was all a family needed, but with four boys and a girl, as well as mum and dad (when he was home), the council had decided to redesign the bathroom and put a toilet in there as well. It was cramped and there always seemed to be a queue to use the loo or the bathroom, but it was much better than going outside to the privy like her old house.

As Moira returned with the coffees, Dave began to feel awkward. He'd got his story worked out on the short walk – he was concerned for her and just happened to be in the area – but it all felt so lame now. What was he going to do? Be honest and say he fancied her? No. And now he daren't look at her, and he was going red, and he'd better sit down because his legs were feeling a bit queasy.

Moira put her cup down and then went over to Dave and leaned over to adjust the standard lamp. Their faces were just an inch or so apart. He turned to say thank you and found his lips brushing against hers. And she did not move away, in fact her lips parted just a little and he kissed her, chastely to begin with, until her arm went round his neck and she dropped slowly to her knees so she was looking up at him, but not seeing anything as her eyes were closed and she was experiencing the most wonderful sensations. Rekindling memories of being with a man.

The kiss ended. Moira rocked back on her knees and looked at Dave as he tried to get his breath back and stop his eyes rolling back in ecstasy.

"Well that was a surprise," she said.

"I'm sorry Moira. I just lost control. I've been thinking of you ever since that day in court. I couldn't get you out of my mind. That's why I'm here really." Dave's words tumbled out as he leaned forward to hold Moira's hands. She didn't seem to be listening and moved forward on her knees to kiss him again, this time not so chastely, and she opened her lips to receive his tongue and feel his hard, chapped lips clamp over hers.

As he moved forward he slipped off the chair and they ended up side by side on the rug, shielded by the thick net curtain and close enough to the red three-seater settee to be hidden from any prying eyes.

Dave's hand moved round her, pulling her towards him and then along until he touched her bottom. Rather than resist, Moira grabbed Dave's shoulder from behind and pulled him closer, and, as his hand moved down her body, she pressed in and opened her legs so she could feel his hand exploring her clothed buttocks.

Moira pulled away and her hands shot up her back, releasing the bra and allowing her breasts total freedom as she pulled her light jumper up and over her head. Then she grabbed Dave again and kissed him forcefully. His right hand moved up and cradled her left breast. Right then it was the nearest he had felt to perfection in a woman in his life. The nipple was as hard as a raisin, but with a smoothness that invited a soft, but firm touch. Moira threw her head back as he kissed her breast and she gasped and then moved back. Her hand moved down and she roughly unclipped her jeans and pulled them down along with her knickers until she was able to kick them off.

Then she grabbed Dave's crotch and gasped with pleasure as she touched his ramrod hard cock. With his help she pulled his jacket off, followed by his shirt, and then easily managed to unbutton his trousers and yank them down, feeling his ramrod leap out and bang against her skin.

"Now!" she mouthed quietly. And Dave did not hesitate, driving himself into her warm, very wet and welcoming moistness. She was already on the verge of orgasm and his powerful thrusts just brought everything forward, and she knew she was about to explode.

Dave realised that this was no time to start slowing things down. He was going to come and he hadn't done that for over a week – and even then it was on his own during his weekly bath. He kept driving forward, kissing Moira until neither of them could breathe, panting as he grabbed her bottom and she grabbed his, pulling him ever inwards.

And then she gasped as he shuddered and moaned, and, at the same time, she felt that delicious tremor that seemed to start with her feet, go up her legs and send star-like shocks from her thighs all over her body. She bucked and bowed to get as much pleasure as she could, knowing that for both of them it would take a little while to recover.

"Well that was an even nicer surprise," Moira said as she gently stroked Dave's hair. He wished he'd washed it that day, but it had been three days and was now a little bit greasy.

"Mmmm, that was wonderful, I ..." But Moira put her finger over his lips as if to say that this was not the time for words of explanation. Just enjoy the moment.

He rolled on to his back and looked across at Moira who was on her side, ankles crossed, resting on her elbow looking at him. What he saw was quite surprising, given Moira's history. She'd kept her body in brilliant shape, despite five kids and a brick shithouse of a husband with an IQ in single figures. She was about five foot five tall, slim, but with what most guys would term "medium" breasts. That meant they were large enough to fill a bra, but still reasonably conical and very exciting and excitable. And she was a natural blonde, as her well-trimmed triangle of pubic hair showed.

Her legs were OK, but he knew why she preferred to wear jeans and trousers rather than the young girl's uniform of micro shorts and skirts. All together, Moira was a very tasty package, but what set it all off was that smiling face. It was as if she was pleasantly surprised at simply being alive, eyes wide open, but not as much as Rita Tushingham, the actress. It was a smile that showed off small, slightly irregular, well-cleaned, white teeth, with cheeks that seemed to fill out a face that was welcoming, bright and very attractive.

"Has that coffee gone cold?" Moira said, not as a question, more a statement of how long they had been lying on a floor that had started as a comfortable and natural place to be, but was now feeling a bit hard and unforgiving. "Let's get some clothes back on shall we, and then I want a few honest answers from you," she said, wriggling back into her jeans and pulling her jumper back over her head. When Dave had managed to get his trousers back up and pulled his shirt on, Moira snuggled on to the armchair with him, and his hand slipped under the jumper to gently caress and stroke her breast.

"I should say I'm sorry," Dave said, "but I honestly can't say it. I've been thinking about you for days now, ever since we saw each other in court."

"And here's me thinking that you simply didn't care," Moira replied. "You really are a sexy man you know, but I'm not really like this at all. I haven't had sex with that pig of a husband of mine, or any man, for the last nine months. Let's not talk about it, let's just snuggle up . . . if you've got time that is and don't have to rush off somewhere and report or whatever."

Dave thought he was a gentleman, but he also knew that this was not going to be one of those deeply romantic interludes. There was her hubby for a start – it seemed a good idea, and a healthy one, not to let him find out what had happened. How would Moira see it? She seemed a bright lady and she wasn't slow in getting things horizontal.

In fact, Moira had already worked it out. Dave was a nice guy, one of the innocents compared to her world of petty thievery, gossip and back-biting, as well as a fair bit of back-stabbing. If he was up for it, he could drop round anytime the kids were away, as long as it was discreet and he didn't start professing all this "love" business. No hearts, no flowers, no weekends away or romantic dinners, no presents, just a damn good shag whenever they both felt like it.

Dave had never met a woman like that. In his life, apart from a long-term fiancée, and it took fourteen months to get inside her knickers – unsatisfactorily for both – and a gradual break-up over the next two years, women had been always wanting something. Usually it was a part of him as a person, including some dreamy ones who started planning for the future after one frigid date, and a lot of the time it was to lighten his thin wallet even further.

Moira was different. She just wanted Dave when she could see him and she made no demands other than affection and satisfying sex. Dave became an infrequent and irregular visitor: enough to satisfy their lust for each other, but not to arouse the suspicions of her neighbours or children.

There lay the dichtotomy that Dave struggled with. The more practical Moira was, the more he wanted to shower her with presents and affection. The solution was to turn the old adage of "hitting them where it hurts" on its head, and find a way of giving her something she would appreciate without wanting to turn it down. All five children had birthdays at least a month apart. Two of the boys had left home, the girl and her closest brother were fairly sporty and had joined athletics clubs – possibly more to get away from an overcrowded home as much as the enjoyment of running – and the youngest, Joe, was bright and took after his mum.

It did not take much to pretend that Moira was working overtime five times a year and then just before Christmas; and it didn't empty Dave's wallet to make sure that there was always enough cash for a present from mum that looked like it had been properly researched – like those running spikes and pedometer for the two middle ones, the Shakespeare and James Joyce books for Joe, and the helpful items of kitchen-ware for the two older boys, even if they were clearly taking drugs and on the borderline of getting into trouble.

Dave stayed in the background, but gradually began to take an interest in the family until it all had to stop when the prison decided that 18 months into a three-year sentence, hubby would be released on licence. Moira was sad, but practical as ever, and told Dave that they would have to cool it totally until he committed another crime and was sent back down – an inevitability, she said, with one of those sad little smiles.

But something had happened inside Nottingham Prison and what came out was, Dave later discovered, a man determined never to go back inside. Within days he had got a job on a farm and then, two months later, he was taken on as a labourer, at a lot better pay, building the bridges for the new inner ring road near the race-course.

Dave resumed his humdrum reporter's life until that morning when they found Joe's body, and that was a hell of a shock. Joe was not a thief. He'd been in the Sixth Form and, last Dave had heard, was heading towards a proper job and career. Being a burglar or petty thief was not like Joe at all.

"So that's how you know the lad we saw this morning, but what are you going to do about it? If he wasn't up on the roof burgling Boots, what was he doing?" asked the young, novice reporter who'd seen his very first dead body that morning.

Dave had no idea, but he was going to find out. What he could not do was tell the police what he knew. With their love of the *Derby Telegraph*, especially the lower-ranking detectives, they would march along to hubby and tell him the full story.

Dave's first thought was to get hold of Moira, but he discounted that immediately. Their past was just that, and he couldn't resurrect it, even as an investigating reporter. But he had to find out why a young lad with a bright future was now lying on the mortuary slab. One solution was to speak to Tom Freeman, a DJ and part-time private investigator. Tom owed him a favour or two.

Tom was built like one of those puppets with a weight at the bottom: you could knock him about, but he would always come back smiling. But only if you knew him well enough, because Tom was pure muscle and had army training – he'd missed National Service by a year, but still joined up because his dad had said it would do him good. It had, but it had also put him off physical violence and turned him to music.

DJ-ing was a great way of getting out and making use of the thousands of records he had acquired over the years. So it was Tiffanys on Friday and Saturday nights and Jaguar Nights, colloquially and better known as the Black Cat or just the Cat, for a more prog rock sound on Thursdays. At Tiffanys he was often accompanied by his long-time fiancée Sandy Banks – taking the micky out of Sandy's name was not advisable – but at the Cat he was invariably without her. Not her sort of music and she didn't like the excessive long hair of almost all the bands, and a lot of the punters.

It was through music that Tom had met Alan Morton, an accomplished jazz drummer, *Telegraph* sub-editor and the editor of the Saturday Page, the newspaper's regular look at Derby's diverse and lively rock, jazz, pop, folk and classical music scene. Tom had known Dave Green a lot longer than he had known Alan and his young acolytes on the Saturday Page. Tom, as an evening entertainer, had been spending most of his days moping around his flat while everybody was at work. Then he'd met a guy called Proctor who ran a detective agency and was looking for people who could carry out some surveillance, and were big enough and tough enough not to be intimidated if they were spotted. For Tom it was a perfect fit.

After a year he'd realised that he didn't need the umbrella and protection of Proctor's Detective Agency, and Proctor himself was getting some of the shittiest, most boring domestic jobs and none of the interesting stuff, like fraud and industrial espionage. That was how he'd first met Dave, a crime reporter who used Proctor as an unpaid sources of news. Over the following few years Dave had been able to hand him some juicy and lucrative jobs, more than enough to buy and run his new Ford Cortina and take Sandy out for those Berni Inn meals she loved . . . and he was sick of.

# 2

————

"SIMON. There's a swimming gala at Belper tonight and the Mayor will be there. You should be able to summon enough skill to cover that," Norman on Newsdesk said to the new-ish reporter. It was the nearest Norman got to a snide remark. He was basically a decent guy working his way quickly to retirement and a move from the three-bedroom detached in Littleover to the two-bedroom bungalow at St Leonard's. At sixty-two and now portly with thick-lensed glasses, his frantic newsroom days were a long way behind him, but he was still a journalist at heart and he felt good about the latest crop of young reporters. Chris Saxon was the best of the bunch with an eye for detail, an enquiring mind, and the ability to get on with most people; Simon Jardine could be something, and his writing style was very good – conversational with, it seemed, every word chosen for impact on the reader – but he was a bit juvenile and was spending more time in the pub at lunchtime than was necessary.

Perhaps a spell under a more experienced journalist, a mentor or tutor, would help his concentration. Failing that he'd be shipped out to the Ilkeston office. That rundown, ex-mining town in a no man's land between Derby and Nottingham tended to have a salutary effect on most reporters.

"OK, Norman. Can I take the office car, I'm not too

sure about buses back this evening." Simon responded, lifting his head up from a copy of NME that had arrived on his desk.

"No. It's Belper and that's on the main A6. There's buses every few minutes," Norman answered almost by rote, then looked down at his meticulously annotated job management table and saw that nobody else was going to need their own transport. "Oh, OK then, but make sure you bring it back safe and sound and it's in Despatch overnight."

The day just got a whole lot better for Simon. He'd passed his driving test two full years ago, but was still not able to afford his own car, and four wheels meant a massive amount of freedom. Plus, if he got in quick enough he could snaffle the Hillman Imp instead of the small van, and the Imp was light and fast. Pity about its rear engine and rear-wheel drive, but he was getting used to that.

Journalism was a natural career for Simon, he'd decided after a year at university. He'd edited the school magazine as well as writing the music and theatre reviews, and he'd turned stilted, fact-strewn prose from the sports fanatics into something worth reading. He loved playing with words on paper, but realised he was not quite quick enough mentally to handle radio interviews. He scraped into university on a geography degree course and it took him less than a month to decide that three more years of academia were not for him. He wanted to be out there in the real world. The one thing that university life in a dying northern town had given him was an entry into the world of music: not just any music, but the prog rock and pop rock that he'd first encountered in the Sixth Form.

Simon was no Adonis, he knew that, but he could charm people, especially older folk and really old people, and, after a few false starts at university he'd lost his virginity to a fat girl who said she was seventeen, and he wasn't going to argue when she was offering him his first full-on sex.

At a smidgeon off six foot tall, Simon was gangly and had a twenty-eight-inch waist and a concave chest, but by the time any girl had got to see his bare torso he was well on his way and could use his hands and fingers to explore their every indentation and excitable protrusion. He did, however, have unusually powerful legs: the result of seven years of nearly five days a week football, athletics, badminton and any other sport that involved running, jumping and generally burning off energy. He'd learned how to swim, but as that meant showing off a chest he was not proud of, he rarely joined in the mixed swimming parties in his teens.

Simon's dress sense was developed round a combination of seeing what others wore and deciding whether he liked the look; an awareness that he was not going to look any better to girls no matter what he wore; and, above all, a conscious decision to spend what little money he had on other things, like booze. The result was a mish-mash of different styles that never quite worked. The Cuban-heeled boots still fitted two years after his mum had grudgingly bought them as a birthday present; the long, tapered collars on his white shirts – bought because the News Editor, he'd heard, liked white shirts on his reporters – were suffering from rotational use as he only had three and only went to the launderette once a week, and his sports jacket and trousers were, to be kind, old-fashioned.

With his first pay packet, augmented by the money his parents had given him, he'd bought a suit. His choice had not gone down well as, combining his youthful, rebellious attitude with a need to conform in the office, his purchase had been a tight-fitting blue denim suit. So, after a brief conversation with Newsdesk, it was back to the old sports jacket and black trousers for most of the week.

The outer Simon bore little relation to the inner man. His ability to get on with people had come from a fairly strict upbringing in a loving family. He could not remember rationing as he was too young, but he remembered the family's first car, the first television and the first proper holiday – to St Ives in Cornwall, and it had been a two-day trip to get there. Simon was innately respectful and his rebelliousness away from home was part reaction to sudden freedom and part a show for his new friends.

Simon was not a chameleon, but he did tend to blend in with many different elements of life. He was as relaxed standing at the door of a church taking the names of dozens of the landed gentry as they entered for a society funeral, as he was lounging backstage at a club with pot-smoking musicians. This trait to his personality, be believed, would help him to be a really good reporter, but in the meantime he knew he had a lot to learn.

Simon's first days at the newspaper had been, for him, eventful and exciting; for Norman, they had been very slightly worrying, but no more so than coping with the usual small batch of would-be reporters fresh out of school, college or university. It was the same old set of problems: enthusiasm, vim and willingness, but without the backing of discipline and that most important asset, the ability to listen first. Simon would be OK, Norman felt. He had imbibed the age-old maxim of newspaper reporting – start the story as if you are telling your mother something and you have to capture her attention, and hold it, in one sentence – with alacrity, and his first, supervised, Magistrates' Court reports showed he had an eye for a story.

Simon had listened intently during one of his first impromptu training sessions when Norman had explained the difference between a reporter and a journalist.

"I don't want any more people on this paper who think they are journalists," he'd said. "I want good, honest, meticulous reporters who report the facts, not make assumptions. Good journalists evolve over the years. When you've got a fair few years' experience, when you've covered the whole gamut of stories and events, and when you have the facts and knowledge to form arguments that stand up to criticism and scrutiny, then you might be able to call yourself a journalist. Until then, be a damned good reporter.

"Oh, and try and stay out of the pub a bit more. We all like a drink, but at your age, no matter what you think, you can't handle it, and it will affect your judgment."

Magistrates' Court was, as usual, boring and the cases were repetitive. There was almost a set format for writing them up, but it was a lot better than his first few weeks in the job, especially that funeral at Breadsall where he and Kevin, another of the new boys, had stood either side of the entrance porch and taken the names of every mourner, and even those whom they were representing.

The job itself wasn't so bad, and he'd been brought up to be respectful of his elders, so asking each of these people standard questions and then checking spellings was not a problem, but the pressure was knowing that if he didn't get every one right then there'd be a complaint and he'd be hauled up before Norman in front of the whole newsroom.

Five o'clock came round and he was able to nip round to the café owned by Pauline, the wife of Alan Morton, Saturday Page supremo. There was always something good on the menu, and for just a few pennies, well, no more than six or seven shillings. Tonight it was a chicken pie with chips and something green, but with lots of gravy, and he wolfed it down. He quickly got back to Despatch, the department so called because it was where all the newspapers arrived from the printing press on the ground floor and were loaded into vans to be despatched to newsagents and street sellers. Speed was important as he wanted to be sure he could pick up the keys for the Hillman Imp.

Belper swimming baths were on the main road through the town and Simon parked round the back. He announced who he was and was ushered to a seat on the tiered viewing area by the side of the pool. He was twenty minutes late and had missed the Mayor's speech praising the swimmers at this, the 1971 Girl Guide Swimming Gala, but there was always the Mayor's Officer to fill him in. This job was going to be another boring one – just a list of names of who took part doing what. He could have picked this up on the phone, or just arrived at nine o'clock and got the lists of winners. His eyes began to droop – some people could stay awake all night, but Simon knew that he could only manage that if he was interested or entertained, and Belper swimming gala was providing neither interest nor entertainment.

Out of the corner of his eye, he noticed that one of the Girl Guides was staying in the pool after the others had got out. They were all standing as a group laughing and chatting, totally absorbed in talking about the routine they had just completed, and all with their backs to the pool. The girl in the pool was doing nothing, just lying face down with her arms outstretched. Something was wrong.

"Excuse me, is that girl OK?" he leaned forward and asked a very plain girl about his age but twice his size, who was sitting directly in front of him. He pointed towards the pool.

"Oh no! It's Sophie!" the girl shouted as she jumped down the four steps from the tiered seats and dived into the pool. She swam powerfully, even in all her clothes and, if truth be told, very elegantly for a girl her size. She grabbed the still, younger girl, hauled her over so she was no longer face down, pulled her with one arm round her shoulders, using the other as a paddle, and in four strokes reached the side of the pool.

Simon turned to his neighbour. "Could I borrow your camera? I'll make sure you get all the prints back, free." Within a couple of seconds, he was standing by the side of the pool taking picture after picture of the two Guides, the younger one being carried out of the pool by her rescuer. Sophie was laid on the ground and an adult in Guide uniform began to press her chest. The youngster was sick – well it sounded as if she was being violently sick – but what came out was clear water. He went back to his seat and asked his neighbour to take the film out.

"I promise you, I'll get all the prints from the film back to you. It looks like the gala has finished a bit early anyway," Simon said, nodding his head towards the pool where there was now still water, with all the activity taking place at one end, as young Sophie sat up, surrounded by older women in Guide uniforms.

The couple nodded and the man, obviously the father of one of the competitors, wrote their address and phone number on the piece of paper that Simon had ripped out of his notebook. Simon was profuse in his thanks as he walked quickly to the organiser who was, by now, waiting for the ambulance she'd called.

"Who was the girl who jumped in?" he asked.

"Oh that's Mary Jones, lives at the top of the hill in Belper. Lovely girl and a great swimmer, but she's too old for this pageant. She's been a great Guide and comes to all our events even though she's about to become a proper Guider. If anybody was going to save a life tonight it would be Mary, she's that sort of a girl."

Brilliant, fantastic. I've been a newspaper reporter for just two months and I've seen my first dead body, covered two great rock bands, and now picked up a good story, Simon thought as he headed back to the car.

"Mr MacMillan wants to see you, so come with me," said Norman as he approached Simon's desk. They walked together into the corridor, turned right and then right again, stopping at the big, closed oak door and knocking, waiting for the standard response. "Enter."

Mr MacMillan had been editor for three years and had taken circulation over the 80,000 copies a night mark for the first time since the Suez crisis. He was also the man who had given Simon the job after he'd gone there just to ask advice about how to get into journalism after eight weeks of rejections from weeklies in the North West where his parents lived.

Norman pushed the door and walked in followed by Simon – gentleman that he considered himself, he was not going to open the door for a lad who had been at the paper for only a few days. He walked across the threadbare carpet into a room that could have been a combination of an undertaker's and a library. Every wall was a bookcase and, apart from the one nearest the massive desk at the far end of the room, was jammed with books, most of which looked as if they had been contentedly gathering dusk for decades. It was dark and moody too. Natural light struggled to enter this inner sanctum and the view – of the town's dirty Market Hall entrance – was obscured by muck that simple washing could not shift.

There was one bright spot: a desk lamp with a green shade flooded a small area of the leather-topped desk with the clarity of a hospital theatre. Without getting up, the editor pointed with his palm upwards towards two chairs on their side of the desk and looked up smiling. It was a smile that Simon remembered from photos of his long-dead grandfather: genuine, broad and kindly and employing the eyes as much as the cheeks, but not an open-mouthed smile.

"Well Simon, have a look at that," he said, swivelling a newspaper page round on his desk so it faced Norman and Simon. "Front page lead and you have only been with us a few weeks. Congratulations are in order. You may think it was just luck that something happened at that little swimming gala last night, but Norman and I know that you showed a lot of good journalistic skill. You got right to the heart of the story, but you also remembered to pick up the competition results. So well done and let's have more like this.

"I know you've enjoyed writing reviews of pop concerts and Alan Morton has spoken highly of you, but I don't want that sort of frippery to take over your life, so Norman and I have agreed that you should link up with Dave Green for a while. Follow him on his enquiries and learn about the way he meets and develops the relationships with police and others. Dave is one of the best crime reporters in the East Midlands and is very well respected, so you should learn a lot. Just one thing though – I suggest you do not follow his wayward path when it comes to drinking. We understand the need to go to pubs and meet people, but there is no need to have a beer in every one – a lemonade will be better."

Norman sensed that the "audience" with the editor was over and he stood up, and Simon followed.

"Thank you sir. I really appreciate it," he said, stumbling over the word "sir", as he was no longer a schoolboy, even if these two older men made him feel that way. The editor stuck out a hand and Simon shook it, turned and followed Norman out of the office.

It was the first of several times that Simon would be asked in to see the editor, but only one of two times he would shake his hand. The other would be when he eventually handed in his notice, and that would be to a different editor, and one he had little respect for.

Dave had already been told about his new "charge" and, while he was not a hundred per cent sure he liked the arrangement, he knew that he needed someone to handle the growing workload. Simon Jardine had seemed like a decent enough lad – and he had demonstrated that he had a good reporter's mindset. But newspaper work was not Dave's highest priority just now. His first job was to meet up with Tom Freeman.

# 3

_____

"You've got a problem then Dave." Tom was loading his records into the back of the Ford Cortina, his pride and joy, and a powerful beast as well. "Nowadays you don't come round unless you've got a problem, and you've come to my house so it must be serious."

"You know the Mahoney family? Live in Chaddesden, the old man has been in and out of nick, but he seems to be going straight now?" Dave asked, knowing that the answer would be affirmative.

"Yes, of course, but things have been very quiet for a while now, ever since Patrick got out of Nottingham. Why are you interested?" Tom's head was lost to sight as he manhandled a wooden box of singles into position.

"The dead body they found at Boots on St Peter's Street was Joe Mahoney," Dave said, and stood back quickly as Tom backed out of the boot, nearly banging his head on the lid.

"No way. That lad was as straight as a die, maybe the only one of those kids who had been straight – well, he'd never really stepped out of line. I sometimes wondered who his father was: he and Patrick may have looked similar, but their personalities were miles apart." Tom leaned back with his hands supporting his lower back.

"You're right and that's why I've come to see you. I don't believe that Joe was up to any funny business and I wondered if you could ask around a bit. Not only have you got better inside contacts with the police, but the criminal fraternity trust you a lot more than they would a local newspaper reporter."

"Something doesn't smell right. Why are you so interested? I heard some rumours about you and Moira while Patrick was inside, but I didn't take any notice. No concern of mine, and I was hardly going to earn a penny or two investigating a relationship between a temporarily single mum and a down-at-heel reporter. Anyway, it was just claims and innuendos and you know me: if I haven't got all the facts I won't touch it. So spill." Tom had moved back and was now sitting on his garden wall, where Dave had found a reasonably comfortable perch.

They'd known each other for over ten years now. Dave had been able to channel some quite lucrative private detective work his way, and their mutual friend Alan Morton had been instrumental in helping Tom get on the road as a DJ as well. Tom had spotted a way of combining his interest in all forms of modern music with his know-how of electronics learned in the army, and Alan Morton had the contacts in the venues.

There wasn't much they didn't know about each other, so Dave decided to tell him everything, including the short-lived fling with Moira Mahoney.

"OK. I'm not going to pass judgment – and even if I was it would be tinged with a little admiration. Moira Mahoney is a tidy piece of womanhood and it seems you've been helping out where it's needed. I'll ask around a bit, discreetly, and get back to you. When's a good time to meet up? I'm working for the next three nights."

Dave knew Tom was a man of his word and he wouldn't be blabbing anything, and he realised that this might be the time to tell him about Simon Jardine.

"That's great. Just one other thing. I've been given a shadow by the newspaper, nothing shady, a young reporter to learn the ropes from me. You probably know him, Simon Jardine?"

"I know Simon. He's one of the best music journos I've met. Maybe not so strong on soul, but there's little he doesn't know about the rock scene, and he's a genuine guy. If you've got a shadow then I don't think you could do any better. I'd trust him, and I've had reason to," said Tom, thinking back to the very few times he had played away with one of the many girls who'd danced as close as possible to his turntables and had made it plain they would be open to some horizontal dancing if he was interested. Simon knew about these transitory conquests, but he never mentioned a word to Sandy; he even covered Tom's back by providing the occasional alibi.

"Why don't we meet up at Tiffanys on Saturday? Simon will be there anyway, he always is if there's no big rock show at the Kings Hall or the college, and I know that the Cat is closed this weekend. You've got two reasons to be there: seeing me as a mate, and having a work chat with Simon."

Dave and Simon had already spoken about working together and there was something resembling mutual respect, despite the age difference. Simon looked up to his journalistic mentor, and Dave had sussed him out as being trustworthy. Perhaps, Dave thought, Simon's involvement in his digging for the reasons behind Joe Mahoney's death would add an extra dimension. Simon was young and, as a part-time pop music reporter, was heavily involved in the lifestyle and "scene" that Joe moved among. They probably shared mutual friends and, if he could help with the right questions, Simon might be able to dig up some relevant facts that the police, with their heavy-handed, half-hearted efforts, would miss.

"He knows. He knows everything I do and what we talked about so we can all be completely open." Dave was leaning against the door in Tom's dressing room at Tiffanys while the band were playing their first set.

Tom looked from Simon, who was flicking through his next session playlist, to Dave and smiled.

"Good, now we can be straight. Joe's dad, Patrick, struck lucky when he came out of prison and he walked straight into a job on a farm owned by one of the local magistrates, Colonel Hamilton-Pocklington – who is also a director of the construction company building the new ring road and bridges over the river in Derby."

Both journalists listened intently as Tom told them the story of Mahoney's employment after leaving prison. So far it wasn't about Joe, but the family connection might become important and it was all background anyway, he said.

"It seemed that Moira met the Colonel when she went for an interview at his home, Morley Manor, and the Colonel promised to see if he could help Patrick get into some gainful employment.

"He was a strong, big man, so heavy farm work was a natural outlet. There wasn't a lot of money in honest farming and the eighty acres in Allenton were becoming a drain on resources, but the farm manager had started to turn things round. The farm was about a mile from the nearest houses along a track with woods obscuring the farm buildings, so any trucks were largely hidden.

The solution to lack of profitability was to take advantage of the draconian laws on dumping waste and, for a hefty fee, allow the ponds and old gravel pits to be filled with waste that would normally have to be licensed and go through expensive cleaning treatments.

"Patrick Mahoney was the ideal man for the job of managing this enterprise. He was desperate for a job and not clever enough to know it was totally illegal. When he did find out, Mahoney said nothing, kept working, and began to use his own initiative to build sight screens, so any visitor to the farm would have no idea of what was really going on.

"Very forward thinking, it turned out, when the local constabulary started investigating 300 gallons of missing paint. The thieves couldn't sell it, but they needed to dump it and the police were on their tail. By the time CID and the uniforms got to the farm, all traces had been removed, the pit covered with manure and a shed that looked as if it had been there for hundreds of years.

"The farm manager got rid of the plods within minutes. Not only was there nothing to see, but he also mentioned that the Colonel would be none too pleased about having business disturbed by the police, and he might have to speak to the Chief Constable, a good friend.

"Patrick's initiative didn't go unnoticed and the Colonel, when he heard, realised that this was a man he could put to better use on the new Pentagon Island construction site.

"So that's all I know at the moment," Tom said. "Mahoney is a foreman and, by all accounts, he is a well-liked boss as well as a conscientious worker. It seems that his loyalty to the Colonel is a bit stronger than his devotion to rigidly staying the right side of the law."

Dave thanked Tom and realised that, with Simon's help, the investigation could work along two parallel tracks. He, with his contacts among the county set and police, could dig discreetly deeper into Colonel Hamilton-Pocklington; Simon, who vaguely remembered meeting someone with that name while he had been on a boozy evening at the Crown Club, could find out more about Patrick Mahoney and the ring road construction project, as well as pursuing the way of life and friends of his now late son.

# 4

—————

DAVE and Simon had ended up in the Exeter Arms. Apart from the best pint of Bass he'd ever had in his life, although four years was not a long beer-drinking life, Simon enjoyed the pub itself. A sort of juxtaposition between the old, black and white pub with its black beams and what seemed like centuries of ingrained cigarette and pipe smoke combined with cheap formica-topped tables. The landlady also looked a bit like his mum on Boxing Day evening – not drunk, but just a little bit merry. The building was set on a building site; the concrete and cement of the new Derby.

All these roads will be gone in a year, Simon had been told by Maurice, the municipal reporter, and he'd heard a strong rumour that the Exeter might be a casualty of what some called progress.

"You're OK with covering Crown Court for the next couple of weeks are you?" Dave asked and, without waiting for the obvious, compliant affirmative, went on: "There are a few people there you should meet, but avoid Pongesbury. As a barrister he would be a better actor; as an actor – well, that's what he sees himself as. He carries that name well. If something has a nasty smell about it, you can be sure Pongesbury is involved.

"The real reason we're here is to set out some ground rules over the Joe Mahoney investigation. The inquest is tomorrow and I'll cover it, but it will just be a matter of identifying the body. The rumour I'm picking up is that young Joe didn't die in that alley, and if that's the case we're looking at murder rather than misadventure," Dave said, finishing his sentence with a long slurp of Bass. He then explained what else he had found out, and where, he thought, Simon could use his journalistic skills.

A contact in CID had mentioned that Joe's father, Patrick, was under some form of surveillance – nothing to do with the death, but he had raised a few eyebrows with his rapid rise in employment status. From farm labourer at Colonel Hamilton-Pocklington's farm – and there were some questions about how he had been hired to work on a farm that was apparently on its uppers – through to Derwent Bank Construction and eventually foreman. One of the problems this CID contact had highlighted was that Patrick Mahoney was rarely seen working at the River Derwent site, even though it was his office base. So far nothing nefarious had been suggested, but the police were keeping a close eye on the development. Derwent Bank had won the contract far too easily, in the opinion of Detective Inspector Ludden, Dave's source of information.

Dave said he would keep following up the traditional channels, but discreetly as he didn't want the newspaper to know what was going on. Simon, meanwhile, could sniff around the council and especially the Planning Department. Dave was convinced that the link between Joe's untimely death and the shady goings-on with the Colonel were the key to this mystery.

Crown Court always finished mid-afternoon, unless there was a jury out, so it was quite straightforward for Simon to approach the Newsdesk and suggest he cover the next Planning Committee meeting. He was young, free and single at the moment – unfortunately – and worked out that if he was in a council meeting he would not be spending money he didn't have in the pubs.

The following evening Simon arrived at the Council House, pen in his pocket and notebook in his hand, to be greeted with what seemed to be a mild panic, with at least one of the secretaries in floods of tears in the committee room. Moving forward to console her, one of the older women shepherded him away.

"Poor Lucy is devastated. She's been asked to fill in for Joe Mahoney, the young lad who died after falling from that roof. They used to work opposite each other and she's taken his death very badly," the matronly type explained.

"So Joe worked here then? How long had he been in the Planning Department? What was his role?" Simon's questions tumbled out and he sucked in his breath to stop himself talking.

"Did you know Joe?" the woman asked. "He'd only been with us for six months and he'd been Mr Moores' right-hand man for the last two of them: they were thick as thieves if you ask me. I don't know what Mr Moores is going to do now."

The last thing Simon wanted was gossip going round about his interest, and this lady seemed to be a contender for "megaphone voice of the council" in that respect. He smiled and said he hadn't known Joe, but he understood how upsetting it must be for everyone, then he took his seat in the Press gallery. A parrot could do this job, he thought, as he marked up the comments against the planning applications as they arose for discussion. It was clearly a put-up job: every application had been decided by the Chairman and all the other councillors were there just to agree.

After ninety minutes, the Chairman, John Moores, called a halt and, as it was only just 9 o'clock, Simon approached the imposing staged area where the committee chairman, his deputy and his officers sat. The Council House was a 1930s modernist monstrosity, built at a time when local authority members were put forward on the grounds of their ability to spend hours in power over their fellow citizens, but ostensibly without being paid for it. It was a system that had developed since the MP was the local landowner and often a peer and he selected a few, normally wealthy, but always high-ranking, dignitaries to make decisions on behalf of the whole town. Inside, the furnishings were solid wood, as befitted the high rank of those who sat in committees and the chamber – or so they thought.

"I was wondering if I might get the chance for an interview about how the new ring road is progressing," Simon asked, looking up at John Moores as he stuffed papers back into a leather briefcase.

"It's ruddy fantastic and it's on time and on budget. What more do you want to know?" the bluff Moores responded, thinking that all Simon wanted was the usual political sound bite.

"I was hoping for a bit more," Simon replied. "With the work now six months on I thought it might be a good idea to have an article on the changing face of the town." Simon had already learned well how to press councillors' buttons, and he knew Moores would take the bait. He was too sure of himself, too confident, and this allowed the arrogance to shine through.

"Yes, yes. Damn good idea. Come to my office, err . . ." he pulled out a large leather-bound diary and flicked through to this month's calendar, "tomorrow morning. That OK?" Simon smiled and apologised. "I'm sorry but Newsdesk say I have to go to Crown Court, but I can be free later."

"Right, right," he was beginning to bluster like a Yorkshire stereotype, rather than the ex-handicrafts teacher from South Lincolnshire that he was. "Come to my office at five o'clock. That all right?"

Simon nodded, smiled, stuck out his hand, and said he would be there at 17.00 hours, hoping that Moores did not see the reference to the twenty-four-hour clock as a very mild piss-take, which it was meant as, just to be a bit disrespectful.

Leaving the Council House, Simon decided that walking home would be better than writing up his boring report, and anyway, he could go in early the next morning. There was nothing in the committee to warrant an early story, and it also gave him the chance to have a pint at the Wagon and Horses on his way.

As he half expected, Dave was propping up the bar chatting to the landlord when Simon walked in, and the fresh pint was in his hands in less than a minute.

"Good meeting?" Dave asked solicitously, knowing that the reply would be short and probably curt. "Bit better than I expected," Simon replied. "There was nothing in the meeting, but I've arranged to interview John Moores early evening tomorrow."

Dave stood up from the bar stool and indicated a couple of wooden chairs in the window with one of those round tables where the legs are always cast iron and always in the place where you cannot stretch your own legs. They sat and Dave began to recount his own detective work, building on the facts supplied by Tom.

Patrick Mahoney's rise to power had been quite meteoric and, if Tom's information gleaned from his CID contact was right, he was heading for an equally hard and fast fall. The Colonel might even join him.

Mahoney had become a trusted employee of Derwent Bank, a firm that, prior to the Derby ring road contract, had done nothing of note apart from building some dodgy housing estates. His history outside the law had quickly become a useful CV as Derwent Bank began to take on sub-contractors and suppliers. Subbies were chosen on two criteria: how much they were prepared to stump up in cash to be given the contract; and how quiet they could keep their business relationship. Suppliers went through a similar process: goods were ordered and received when they were needed, but twice the amount of goods appeared for the money paid. If the receipt was a little woolly in terms of quantities, Derwent Bank had an accountant good enough to persuade the Inland Revenue that everything was above board.

Everything had been going smoothly until Patrick found an aggregate supplier from his home country – home being a loose description of the Ireland his father had taken him to when he about ten years old and had never gone back to. O'Malley had a similar pedigree, but he was able to find aggregates that fitted the bill for about half the price. He was a one-man operation with no wife or kids, and saw no reason to complicate his life with outside influences such as needy women. If he wanted a woman he could nip down to Leicester, where he was not known, and pay for one for an hour or two.

O'Malley was no fool. He knew the scam that

Derwent Bank was pulling and he had every intention of meeting them half way – his half way – and that meant Derwent Bank paying more, and him, as far as the taxman was concerned, receiving less.

"This O'Malley character seems to have gone missing, but nobody is that worried. As far as our friends in the police are concerned he had no criminal record or, in fact, any record. He lived in a caravan somewhere, but nobody knows where and he drove a Land Rover that was falling to bits," Dave finished his story.

"There's obviously a link between the council and Derwent Bank and I'd take bets on Moores knowing more than he should. What should I ask him tomorrow? Do you think Joe Mahoney was involved as well as his dad?" Simon asked and pondered at the same time.

"It's too much of a coincidence," Dave replied. "I'm not saying that Joe was involved in the shenanigans of contracts and stuff, but he was close, too close, to John Moores. When you do the interview start with the stuff that's going to please him, like how much this is going to change the face of the town, and you can even mention the plans for Derby to become a city and what the new roads and bridge will do to make this even more certain. Then you can subtly suggest that, while he is at the fulcrum, his choice of people around him has been fundamental in turning dreams into reality. I know it sounds like bullshit, but just watch his chest blow up – and listen to him telling you all those little confidences. The bigger you make him feel, the happier he'll be to let slip the details that we're looking for."

Simon was going to have an early night, so he finished the pint he'd bought, squaring the round with Dave, and headed home.

# 5

---

Tim Hamilton-Pocklington was a wealthy man, so others thought. He had the flash motor, a Rolls-Royce Silver Shadow – and would have bought the Silver Mist as a joke if the company had not changed its name when they were told that 'Mist' in Germany, a good, strong market, translated as 'shit' – and a smart house in the country. But he also had some of the less savoury trappings of success that came with what was termed "old money", or family inheritance.

First off there was the fact that, while he was nominally the owner and resident of Morley Manor, it was mortgaged up to his eyeballs, and he could never sell it anyway. He was only living there until he died, when the house would revert to the trust of which his sister, Agnes, and her two brats were also signatories. Agnes was not going to let him forget it. There were enough pictures and bits of silver in the house to make him a tidy profit, but Agnes had done a full inventory every three years for the past nine years, when his mother had finally thrown off her dementia and stopped breathing – and nagging. In effect, all his assets were locked up as securely as if he was in prison – and the rent from the three farms was only just enough to cover the running costs of the estate and a bit to live on.

The other problem was that he was a homosexual, and had known it since he was about nine years old, some thirty years ago, but he wanted to keep it his little secret. In fact, while he showed no interest in a long-term relationship, he was a lot happier living the lie, playing the role of an upstanding, ex-military bachelor, and he had no problem finding attractive women to be his partner at social activities. It's just a game of pretend like I've always had to play, he thought.

Real love came in short bursts and he paid for it. Holidays in San Francisco, the growing gay scene in Bali, and weekends in Amsterdam where he could buy rent boys who never had to know his name or who he was, just some good-looking Englishman. Agnes knew, of course, but there was no way she was going to air the family laundry in public, not if she wanted her two brats to inherit Morley Manor without him kicking up a high-profile fuss.

There'd been a slight problem with Moira Mahoney when she'd come for the cleaning job interview and seen the young Dutch gardener giving him a quickie blow job in the conservatory, but he reckoned he'd sorted that by offering her husband a job when he got out of prison.

Patrick Mahoney had done well, especially over that paint business at the farm, and when the contract for the new ring road over the river had been awarded and Derwent Bank Construction had won it, he began to believe the company PR consultant's own press releases – that he was a pretty good, shrewd businessman.

The call from Clive Browne had not been totally unexpected and he was happy to agree to a meeting at the County Club near Nottingham Castle. It was his sort of club: doormen with deference; a polite, if slightly obsequious, cloakroom attendant; a barman who saw himself as a servant, a sort of butler if you will, rather than the proprietor; and comfortable, old leather chairs. The only people who got in were old money, new money and guests who had to follow a strict code of conduct and dress; plus, the only women were butch dykes or hard-nosed legal types – men in women's clothing he surmised.

Clive Browne was "new money", but amassed over twenty years ago when he was in his twenties. The Colonel never questioned how a railway foreman could become a millionaire by the time he was twenty-five. Everybody had a past and a few secrets and Clive was a very hospitable host at his dinners and the shooting parties on his estate in North Leicestershire.

The smile seemed genuine enough as Clive rose from his chair to greet the Colonel. "Good to see you again Tim. You look rather bronzed and healthy. Been somewhere exotic and debauched?" he said as he motioned the Colonel into the armchair next to him and pointed a finger skywards to attract the barman's attention.

The Colonel blushed, remembering the sunbed and following massage in San Francisco a month ago. "Thank you. Yes, I feel pretty good. Business is fine at the moment, and when the first payments for the Derby roads job come through I might manage to profess a small profit for a change," he said, ordering a bottle of Chateau Guey, a Graves that he had picked up on a week or so ago. It was not too old a wine, and was chosen because it was mid-priced. Clive smiled: he knew every trick in the book, and he also knew that Tim Hamilton-Pocklington was as much a wine critic and lover as he was a camel rider. Ah, snobbery: a foible he knew well how to manipulate to his advantage.

The pair chatted amiably for about five minutes. Tim was slightly more effusive, Clive smiling but a little more taciturn, and looking back Tim realised that he did not remember a word of what Clive said, it was just a stream of nonenties and nonsense. Eventually the conversation returned to the Derby project and Clive sat back and steepled his fingers.

"It was about the Derby job I wanted to speak to you," he said. "I'm very pleased that Derwent Bank won the contract, but you do realise that it was down to me, don't you?"

The Colonel raised an eyebrow. As far as he was concerned the tendering process had been all above board. He'd taken a couple of guys from the Planning Committee out for a meal, made sure that their tickets for the Executive Box at Derby County had arrived at their homes, and organised that evening in Birmingham where some cleaned-up whores had joined them later, but that was just normal business, certainly on a contract of this size.

"Yes," Clive explained. "The chairman of the Planning Committee is well known to me, a family friend you might say. He and I go back a score or more years and he owes me big time. So a few small favours are in order, I think."

The Colonel sat back as Clive outlined his plan for reimbursement of the favours he talked about. On a £25 million contract Tim was expecting to make a legitimate profit of £2 million, and then there were the rake-offs from the suppliers and sub-contractors, and that would treble his profit. But Clive had other ideas.

First off, the £2 million written into the contract would go direct to the Colonel and Derwent Bank, less a twenty per cent referral fee. Then Clive, with his powerful and extensive network of materials suppliers and specialist sub-contractors, would take control of all third-party arrangements.

"It's called working together, Tim," Clive concluded with a smile. "Remember, this is just one contract and if we're working together then I can see a lot more coming your way. There's a new shopping centre outside Leicester on the cards and the new Labour government is jammed full of poor people who are having trouble living the high life on their MPs' salaries."

The Colonel had lost some of his bronze colour. In the space of a twenty-minute conversation he had seen a nailed-on £6 million inflow of cash reduced to £1.6 million. This was Derwent Bank's biggest ever contract win; he had plans to let it run for at least a couple of years without the tedium and effort of looking for more work; and it was a big step forward in his plans to retire in five years to that extensive bungalow in Bali with the availability of all those young, attentive Dutch boys.

He was in a hole and he knew he could not afford to dig any further. There were three choices: he could argue and fail – Clive Browne was the biggest businessman he knew; he could negotiate to see if he could get some more of the action; or he could simply accept the offer and recognise that he had been beaten fair and square. In the end he chose a fourth option. "I'm shocked. What you've said leaves me very little room to manoeuvre. I need to think. Can I get back to you in a few days?" he said, looking into his now nearly empty second glass of wine.

Clive had known all the options and was grateful that the Colonel had not tried to negotiate or argue. He had all the aces: no amount of words was going to change the fact that the Derby ring road project, instead of being a Derwent Bank Construction contract, was now a partnership, but a silent, secret partnership, and a very profitable one for him.

"Yes, of course Tim. Today is Tuesday, so I expect your call to my office on Thursday morning. When Sandra answers the phone and starts to grill you, just say you're responding to the County Club meeting. She's a brilliant gatekeeper, but it does tend to put some people off." Clive leaned across and refilled the Colonel's glass, but left his, previously filled with tonic water and a lemon slice to look like a gin and tonic, empty.

"Look, it's been great meeting up and having a chat, but I have to pick the wife up from the centre of town, she loves those boutique shops under the Council House. We'll speak on Thursday," Clive said as he rose from the chair, signalled to the barman to put the drinks on his tab, shook Tim's hand firmly, and walked into the vestibule.

Tim finished his wine in two gulps and sat back, exhausted. He felt as if he'd been screwed and could see no way back. If this was a card game then Clive Browne was not just playing with marked cards, he held every ace, and Tim could not afford to stack. He was in too deep. That £6 million – well, most it – had already been earmarked. It was more than his retirement fund, it was cash flow and living expenses. The difference between £6 million and £1.6 million wasn't just a chasm, it was a whole world as far as he was concerned, and he couldn't let Browne, that ex-railway navvy, get away with it. But solving the problem was going to take time and careful thought, and he only had two days to come up with a plan.

By the time his thoughts were starting to gel, Tim had finished the bottle of wine and followed it with four large whisky and sodas, but he was fine, and driving back along the A52 would be no problem.

# 6

COLONEL Hamilton-Pocklington hadn't remembered much about the drive back from Nottingham. He'd stuck to the A52 and then gone through Spondon rather than his usual country route. He wasn't pissed; he could take his drink and, in fact, he thought he was better at speed when he'd had a couple of snifters. When he'd got home, just in case the police were on his tail, he'd had a couple more large single malts, and slumped in front of the fire. He wasn't sure if Derbyshire police were using these new breathalyser kits, but he wasn't prepared to risk it.

An hour later he awoke and realised that the meeting with Clive Browne had not been a nightmare. It had been real and he was under pressure, but there was a solution, or at least part of one, and the Irish aggregates guy figured high in that solution. He called Patrick Mahoney and said he wanted a full up-date on all contracts, and a parallel inventory of the black contracts – those that he was beginning to base his future on. If he could accelerate payments, cut a few corners, and get money in the bank, he could call Browne and tell him that he reluctantly agreed with being royally ripped off by the bastard.

By his reckoning, if he could get £2 million into his accounts by the end of this month that would leave Browne with £2.4 million, with the £1.6 million that had already been agreed as his legitimate profit.

Tim Hamilton-Pocklington called Clive Browne's office and, true to the financier's word, got through with the minimum delay.

"Ah, Tim, good to hear you," Browne said.

"Clive, can you take this off loudspeaker please, I don't want anybody else to hear what we say – and you're not taping this call are you?" The Colonel had already detected the echo from Browne not picking up the handset and he knew he liked to listen with both ears. When he'd done it in the past, with Tim in his office, it had looked very powerful and controlling, but this time he wanted a one-to-one using the handset.

Browne picked up the receiver and leaned back. "All right, you've got my undivided attention, so talk away."

"I've been thinking over what you were saying and it's going to make life very difficult for me."

"Stop there Tim. You know you're going to agree, you know we're not negotiating so let's get that straight. Once you say so, then I'm sure we will be able to work very closely together, and I did say that there are some quite fat, lucrative jobs for us to look at, didn't I?"

The Colonel stared at one of the paintings in his office. A guy with a tall, flat-topped hat, with a servant girl in front of him and what must be his wife behind him. Umm, he thought, here's a guy facing trouble whichever way he goes – a bit like himself.

"Yes, you know I'm going to agree. You've given me no choice, but I was hoping for a bit more money. The way you've set it out, you get sixty or seventy per cent and I'm left with the dregs."

Browne raised his eyebrows. "Tim, Tim, these are not

dregs. This is real money in your hand that I've worked hard for, and do remember this is all a precursor to the awarding of a lot more contracts."

The Colonel gripped the telephone receiver hard. "Like I said, it's not quite what I wanted, but if it's all I'm going to get then we have an agreement."

Browne smiled, the smile of a successful predator. "Good, that's done, and our word as gentlemen is our bond. What I can do is advance you some of the project profit to tide you over. Not the full £1.6 million, after my commission, but maybe half a million. Is that OK?"

It was not a question and the Colonel knew it was a final offer. Browne did not gamble or bargain: as a final offer, to be fair, it was not a bad one. "Do I have to sign anything or is this all down to us as gentlemen?" he asked, knowing the answer before the thought had left his lips.

"I think it's best if we don't put pens to paper, don't you? Bits of paper tend to form an uncomfortable trail. Just get your bank account details, or wherever you want the money to go, to Sandra and she'll sort everything out," Browne said as he sat back. The pair said their goodbyes and both put down the phone.

"Patrick I need to meet you, but not here. Don't come to the Manor. I'll see you this evening about six o'clock at the Post House by the motorway – and get changed into something half respectable, they won't let you in if you're wearing a hard hat and boots," the Colonel said when he phoned Derwent Bank's ring road project site office.

Mahoney was a bit peeved. It was three days before Christmas – his first with Moira and the kids since he had got out, and the first time for many years that he had been able to spend legitimate money on presents and a tree – and now the boss was demanding an evening meeting.

Deep down Mahoney had always known that his job with the Colonel would come down to this. In a way he was surprised it had taken so long. When he took the farm job he was overjoyed at getting paid a very fair wage – £25 a week was a lot more than any labourer he'd known – and he'd actually enjoyed the dodgy business with the paint. Getting one over on the plods was always a pleasure.

Derwent Bank Construction had been even better. He seemed to have a natural aptitude to handling heavy machinery like dumpers and dozers, and the cranes were not too difficult – a little bit fiddly and he was not as accurate as the trained drivers, not after a couple of months, but he could lift and carry with them.

Where he felt he was at his best though was as a leader of men. He was bigger than any of the others, certainly stronger, and when he hit something it usually stayed hit. The little argument on his first week had been unfortunate, but the guy was not being respectful to the Colonel and the spade across his back was just meant as discipline. The fact that he was now off site and would not be working for a few months was tough, but since then none of the other guys had argued with anything.

He had a natural rapport with the Colonel: he had the brawn and muscle, the Colonel was the brains and the money man – you don't drive a Rolls-Royce unless you are smart.

He saw the Colonel as he walked from the car park – hiding the old Bedford van as far back as possible so it would not look so stupid parked next to the Sierras, the car of choice for the travelling sales executives who seemed to populate the hotel. By the time he'd got to the table a pint of gassy beer had already been delivered and was sitting beside the Colonel's whisky. He didn't like beer when he was driving, and he certainly didn't like the gassy stuff they served in these types of hotels, but he took a sip after sitting opposite the Colonel.

"We've got a bit of a problem. There's a guy in Nottingham who's muscling in on the ring road job and he plans to take a barrow full of cash that should rightly be coming to me and Derwent Bank," the Colonel explained.

"That's simple boss. I can handle it. Where does he live? I can just drive round, pay him a visit, and have a little chat," said Mahoney, slightly puffing out his chest and allowing a massive bicep to tighten his shirt sleeve as he picked up his pint.

"No," the Colonel replied with a tight smile. "This guy has more protection than the Queen, and even if you do get to him your life expectancy, and mine, will not last to Christmas. There's another way of handling this problem, but I'll need your loyalty and support."

Mahoney relaxed and shrugged his shoulders. He knew only one way of sorting out a problem that was actually a person, but if the Colonel knew better, he'd listen.

"First off I need you to get all the files together from all the sub-contractors and we'll need up-front payments, without paperwork, from all of them based on the arrangements we have already made. These do not go through their books or ours.

"I then need to have a close look at what this

O'Malley is doing. He may not look like much or throw his money around, but I am absolutely convinced he is ripping me and us off somehow. Have a look round at the other aggregate suppliers and see what they can offer, but do it quietly. I don't want this coming back to me or Derwent Bank and biting us on the bum."

Mahoney nodded slowly. There was nothing illegal in dealing with paperwork or asking questions and he could tell Moira that he was working closely with the Colonel, that it was all big business and very hush-hush. That would impress her.

The meeting was obviously over. The Colonel was saying nothing and just sent him over to the bar to get another large whisky – he'd declined another pint of froth. When he got back he remained standing, handed over the glass, and said that he should be going back to his family and that he would start work first thing the next day.

Early the next morning, Mahoney was in the site office before the physical work began. After spending two hours laboriously going through the contract agreements, and reading was not his strongest suit, he got a brief telephone call from the Colonel saying that he was going away for a few days and would be back early in the New Year. Mahoney smiled. He was not best pleased at the headache he'd got from looking through the papers, but it looked as if his family Christmas was on – for the first time for many years.

Moira deserved something a bit special and she'd been hankering after one of those heated trolleys on casters, Hostess they were called, he thought, and the kids were not a problem. Money would have to do because he didn't know what they wanted and for the first time ever he had been able to save up £80, so a fiver each would still leave more than enough for a few bottles of bubbly and a night out or two.

Moira was busy on Christmas Eve doing all the preparations for when all five kids came round the next day. David and Martin had left home a couple or three years ago, and the two sporty types, Mary and Patrick Junior, plus Joe, the clever one, were still living at home, but he rarely saw any of them so it would be good to have them round for Christmas dinner. Rather than be at a loose end, Mahoney decided he'd walk down to the Crown Club in Spondon. It was only ten minutes and the beer was OK, none of this gassy stuff, and there was often a jazz band on that he could either listen to or talk over.

Jim Finney was on piano when he arrived – now that was a musician. None of this prog rock stuff, just really good swinging jazz. He got a pint and sat at a table where there were a couple of youngsters.

"This chair taken?" he asked as he put his pint down.

"No that's fine. And Happy Christmas to you," the lad said smiling through a beery face. "I'm Simon and this is my friend, Melanie."

"I'm Patrick. Has Jim been on stage long?" Mahoney said and nodded his head towards the green curtains.

"About ten minutes," Simon replied. "I'm covering it for the *Derby Telegraph* so don't be surprised if I take a few notes. My boss, well one of them, is on drums, that's Alan Morton."

Mahoney nodded to them both and settled back to enjoy his pint. He'd picked a good place to sit. Sharing a table with two people who were interested in the music and themselves meant that they would not be bothering him. On some evenings out he'd met people from his past and he was a world away from them now. They were in dead-end jobs or into petty thieving; he was a fairly well-paid executive businessman, or that's what he'd been told by the Colonel.

"So what do you do?" Simon asked.

Shit. Questions, bloody questions, but he seemed harmless enough. "I work on the new ring road project. I look after the materials suppliers and sub-contractors," Mahoney replied with a touch of pride. It had been an innocent enough question and a straightforward reply.

"Great," Simon said. "That's a big job and it'll change the town dramatically." He raised his pint and tipped it slightly towards Mahoney, ending the conversation pleasantly, and mused that this guy would have made a frightening bouncer. If I was on that job I'd be scared shitless if he came along to inspect my work, he thought.

Two pints was enough for Mahoney. He wasn't used to boozing and he had to go back and be a man and a husband to his wife. He smiled inwardly, knowing that he would have no trouble getting a hard-on with Moira. She'd kept her good looks and shape, even after five kids, and she was still a bit of a wild kid in bed.

Christmas, Boxing Day and then New Year went without a hitch. He'd had a few cross words with David and Martin, but that was to be expected. Mid to late twenties and they thought they knew everything. He'd got a little bit cross when Martin mentioned that this was the first Christmas they'd all had together because the head of the family had been in and out of prison, but he'd sorted that by explaining that he was now a fully legit businessman earning good money. He supposed that the "fully legit" bit would not stand up to too much scrutiny, but what he was doing was just what every businessman did – not break the law, per se, just bend it a fair bit.

For the first week of January he had had to run the ring road site himself as the Colonel was still away somewhere exotic, San Francisco he thought he remembered. Then, on the 10th, he breezed back into the office.

The Colonel liked 'Frisco. Where Bali seemed to be full of young boys willing to try anything, and always smiling, loving, touchy-feely, and seemingly with no ties, the money question always had to be answered and agreed first. In San Francisco it was a more adult experience. He was seen as a posh Englishman and could take his pick of some very muscly young men. He was also able to stay with some like-minded acquaintances who'd moved to the outskirts of the city in the mid-Sixties. Where Bali was young, brown, smooth bodies, 'Frisco was more manly with dark leather jackets. He felt sated after nearly two weeks in the Californian winter sun, but now it was back to problem-solving on a major scale.

Mahoney, given that he was no academic genius, had done well. The Colonel had given himself a month, or to the end of January, before he took the relevant books over to Clive Browne. By then, he hoped, O'Malley would be out of the equation and some of the big sub-contractors would have paid up, so Browne would be taking a lot less than the £2 million or thereabouts he was hoping for.

He needed to sort the O'Malley situation out face to face. He'd understand business and he could always go and handle some other contract somewhere, but right now he wanted him out of Derby. Mahoney had already gone direct to O'Malley's suppliers of aggregates and they'd agreed to sell direct to Derwent Bank, at very good rates. Mahoney could set up the meeting here, but it would be, on the face of it, just the two of them, with Mahoney very close if things got physically unpleasant.

They agreed to meet on the Monday of the last week of January. It was bitterly cold and snow was forecast, and by 6.30 it would be very dark.

"Welcome Mr O'Malley, and thank you for coming here. I'll not beat about the bush. We won't be needing you after the end of this month. I'm sure you understand, it's just a business decision," the Colonel said as he waved O'Malley to the wooden upright chair in the small office.

"I'm sorry Mr Hamilton-Pocklington, we seem to have a communications problem here," O'Malley said, rolling the double-barrelled name and missing the prefix of Colonel to make sure he got the message of disrespect across fully.

"If you check the contract it states that I will be supplying you with all aggregates and other specified materials for the life of the ring road project. I think that's clear and there seems little point in continuing this conversation." O'Malley stood up, and the Colonel waved him back into his seat.

"That contract is only as good as the paper it's written on. If we stop paying you there is little you can actually do, and I'm sure that, with the purchasing arrangements you have in place, you won't want to take legal action or bring in the police. Let's just shake hands as businessmen and call it a day." The Colonel got out of his leather high-backed chair and was immediately and forcefully pushed back into it by O'Malley.

"It's you that doesn't understand," he said. "There's a slight change to the contract and purchasing agreement. As of now I want paying up front for the next three months' materials or you'll get nothing through to this site. You may think you can approach my suppliers, but I have a lot more holds on them than you can even dream about. They do what I say, not what you beg." O'Malley moved towards the door, but by then the Colonel had turned off the desk lamp – the pre-arranged signal to Mahoney.

O'Malley strode outside towards his Land Rover and the Colonel shouted: "Mahoney! Stop him!"

Mahoney was in the control cab of the crane and swung the bucket round, planning to drop it between O'Malley and his Land Rover, but his controls were still not that good. As the heavy steel bucket swung down it clipped O'Malley on the head and he fell forwards and didn't move. The Colonel ran down the path.

"You've killed him you mad bastard," he shouted up to Mahoney. A quick glance at the damage the crane bucket had done was enough: O'Malley was not going to go any further with a massive chunk taken out of his head and brain oozing on to the path.

"Shit. What are we going to do?" Mahoney said after he'd clambered out of the cab and run down to the dead body.

"What's this 'we'?" the Colonel replied, knowing that he was in the mess just as much as his employee. He looked around and surmised that they were totally alone, no untoward sound had been created and, if they acted reasonably quickly, they could keep it that way.

"How full of concrete is that bridge support stanchion?" he asked, pointing at one of the major supports for the bridge over the River Derwent.

"Not very. They started it today and we've got more concrete ready for the night shift that starts in about an hour or so," Mahoney replied.

"Right. Get back in that crane and dump the body into the form, then put another six foot of concrete over it. I want nobody to see the body or any evidence at all. Then you can wash down this gory mess," he said, pointing to the blood and brains that were staining the path.

"What'll we do with the Land Rover?"

"Take it to the farm at Allenton and sink it forever in one of the ponds. I'll come and pick you up about 10pm, that should give you enough time to sort the mess out here and get to Allenton, and finish the job. "I've got to get all those papers out of here so there's no evidence that we ever met O'Malley."

Mahoney's adrenalin was racing. He got back in the crane and, using the grab of the bucket, picked up O'Malley's body, then swung it round until it was over the narrow square where the concrete had been poured in. This time he was very careful. He had to be accurate, and O'Malley's body dropped like a sack on to the setting concrete below. He then jumped out of the cab and started the pump from the concrete mixer, which had been revolving slowly all the time to prevent it setting. He allowed the thick heavy liquid to pour in, covering the body completely and leaving no trace that a human was in there at all.

Driving the Land Rover was easy, much easier than his van, and he got to the farm without any hold-ups or, it seemed, the attention of other road users. One Land Rover looks just like any other. Sinking it was not a problem. There were enough heavy waste materials around and he knew that the pond was deep enough. As he pushed it down the slope the pond looked like the open mouth of some monster, hungrily sucking the vehicle under the water and then quickly settling back into a smooth, innocent surface.

It was only when he sat back and waited for the Colonel to turn up that he realised the enormity of what had just happened. OK, he'd been a petty thief and he'd got a criminal record as long as most people's arms, but he'd never killed anyone. It had been an accident, and then he'd just been following orders, he thought, but the shaking and sweating were not going to stop.

He was pleased to see the Colonel appear dead on time. He'd never been in a Rolls-Royce, and he wasn't that impressed. It smelt rich and leathery, and there was no sound from the engine, but he remained terrified.

"Pull yourself together man," the Colonel said as he swung round past the side of the Derbyshire Royal Infirmary. "It's done and you can't undo it. What matters now is that we both act naturally and get back to work."

The Colonel explained that O'Malley would not be missed. No one knew where he lived, except that it was in a caravan he owned somewhere. He had no family and, as far as he was aware, no friends. Nobody would come looking and even if they did, there was no evidence that O'Malley had been to the site office.

He would speak to the suppliers and say that

O'Malley had agreed to the new plans and he'd not been seen for a few days. These were business people and all they wanted to know was that they would get the agreed sums on time.

# 7

$D$ERWENT Bank was doing well. The arrangement with Clive Browne had turned out better than the Colonel had imagined. While he had connections with the landed gentry and titled folk – the sort of people he dined with – Browne linked up with people like John Moores, head of planning for Derby Council. It was a combination that boosted his ego as he could be seen as head of a successful business as well as one of the established aristocracy. The result was that the contract seemed to be growing and extending. Instead of seeing an end to construction in a couple of years when the bridge section taking the road from the Paragon Island into town at the Cockpit was finished, Browne had got Moores talking about extending the work right to St Helen's House on one side and then continuing past the Infirmary to sweep round to join Burton Road on the other side.

It seemed that Derwent Bank did not have to worry about re-tendering for all this work. Browne had simply got the council, well Moores, to see it all as extensions to the original job.

The only problem he had was with Mahoney. He was still a loyal employee, but ever since that business in January he'd been a bit withdrawn, and it meant that he'd had to spend more time at the site rather than just leaving Mahoney to make sure everything was working well and on schedule. He'd also been a bit lax in his timekeeping, which was very unusual, but the Colonel knew he was stuck between a rock and a very, very hard place. Mahoney knew too much, was in too deep, and could not be allowed out of the company. He certainly could not sack him.

February seemed to pass by in a blur for Mahoney. He was still in deep shock over the death of O'Malley and he spent every day waiting for a blue light and knock on the door. He'd very reluctantly been to see a doctor who had given him some tablets after diagnosing some form of depression – but he wasn't depressed, just scared shitless – and he had been waking most nights at about four with a headache and stomach cramps.

Evenings had been the worst, though. Stuck in the house with the woman he loved and two or three young people he was growing very proud of, and his deep guilt about O'Malley meant he could not say anything. The way out was to go for a walk and his evening walk usually took him past the obnoxious smells of the plastics factory in Spondon on his way to the Crown Club. He hated that chemical smell from the factory and the wind always seemed to be blowing west, taking it deep into Chaddesden.

For a man who'd seen the error of his ways, as the chaplain at Nottingham Prison had said countless times, and almost stopped drinking, Mahoney knew he was sliding back down the path to his old habits. From a maximum of a couple of pints, his trips to the Crown and the number of pints he drank were gradually increasing. Mike, the landlord, was pleased to see a frequent regular – business had dropped off apart from

Thursday nights, Sunday lunchtime jazz, and the bingo on Friday and Saturday nights.

Joe got himself a job with the council in March and started working in the Planning Department under John Moores, so his father had suggested a celebratory pint. It had been readily accepted. Joe saw in his father someone who had travelled a very rocky road from being a thief and being sent to prison several times when he and his siblings were young, to a man with a good job, using his obvious talents, and getting paid a fair whack. Mahoney did not know it, and would not have accepted it if he did, but his youngest son was proud of him. The big difficulty was that, as hard as he tried, he did not see him as a father figure. No bond had been formed at an early age.

For Patrick every day was becoming the same: drive the Bedford van to the site office for 7.30, although a few times he was a bit late because of his morning headaches; walk round the site and check on the different projects; lunch at the Exeter Arms, usually on his own, but sometimes with some of the junior foremen willing to buy a drink for a morose mountain of a man who said very little; back home at 6pm for a tea that never varied week to week, but in fairness was well cooked and full of meat; and then a walk to the Crown until closing time.

"It's your birthday, so where would you like to go?" Moira asked one morning as they were both preparing to leave for work. She was hoping he'd say the new Chinese that had opened on the shopping arcade next to Macfisheries. He'd liked experimenting with foreign food and been a big fan of the Indian near the station, and she'd heard some good reports.

"Don't care really. I'm not into birthdays any more, especially my own," Mahoney replied, fighting off the effects of a particularly bad headache and feeling those stomach cramps again. "I'm not interested," he added as he pushed past her to get out of the front door and into his van.

Moira shrugged her shoulders. She was getting used to these depressive moods, but it didn't mean she liked them. For months after starting work with the Colonel, Mahoney had been a different man, a proper husband, and now he seemed to be drifting back to his old self. They hadn't made love for months. He was too tired, too lazy, too headachy, or, as she suspected most of the time in combination with all his other excuses, too drunk. Still, she'd make him a nice big tea tonight and see if that made him feel any better.

Mahoney spent the day making life difficult for everybody he came in contact with. From being a trusted working mate, albeit one with the constant ear of the boss, he was changing. Last autumn you could have asked him for anything and he would have thought about whether it was at least half reasonable. The younger guys were getting time off to go to Wilmorton College for training as part of the new apprenticeship schemes, and the older ones with families were able to take some time off if there was a problem at home. Now, Mahoney just grumped and picked holes in everything he could. The youngsters were OK – he didn't seem to care if they were on site or not – but the middle-aged blokes, the ones who knew what they were doing, had a hell of a time. Mahoney still had the ear of the boss, but this time he was using it to sack whoever he wanted, depending on the mood he was in.

He was dreading this birthday. Moira would make a special effort, the kids would be round that evening, and he hated it. They just didn't realise the heavy burden he was carrying – he'd killed a man for God's sake. It wasn't his fault really, just an accident, but then he'd done what the Colonel said, got rid of the body and all the evidence. No. He wasn't going straight home, he'd have a pint or two first.

He slid into his seat at the Crown. The last few weeks had seen him getting in earlier and earlier, so getting one of the precious bar stools was easy. He motioned to Mike to get him a beer. Mike ostentatiously looked at his watch to say, without using words, "You're early", but Mahoney wasn't in a joking mood and just waited for his pint, downing over half in one go and then leaning back and stretching his muscles.

He knew he could not be so self-centred all night, and the first rush of alcohol calmed him down. It was an effort, but he turned his mouth into a smile and pushed the empty glass towards Mike.

"Sorry about that. It's been a tough day," he said as Mike pulled the new pint.

"Yeah, OK," the landlord replied, "but you've been a bit moody for a few weeks now. Anything you want to talk about?" Mike Madeley was a good landlord and had spent a career dealing with people. His last job had been as manager of a cinema in Nottingham and he'd only left because it was part of a massive international group and they were bringing in management styles that would, in his opinion, kill the personal touch. Running a pub or club was a better choice, and he had proved exceptionally good at it since he took over the Crown Club eighteen months ago.

"No, everything's fine. It's my birthday today and I just don't feel in a mood to celebrate. That's why I'm here with a miserable old bugger like you instead of doing bunting and champagne at home with the wife and kids," Mahoney said, visibly relaxing as the beer took effect.

"Happy birthday," Mike said. "This one's on the house." And the third pint of a so far very short evening was put in front of Mahoney. Mike turned away to serve two new customers and, pulling their drinks, he noticed that Mahoney had slipped into his now frequent morose state, slouched forward with the beer glass protected by his wrapped-around, well-muscled arms, his head almost level with the glass and his chin only a few inches off the bar top. It wasn't an intimidating pose, more that of a sad, broken man, but you still wouldn't ever argue with Mahoney. He looked malignant and, even with a few beers in him, you knew he could pack a punch.

Three hours, and several pints, later Mahoney got off the bar stool and handed his van keys to Mike.

"Best if I don't drive," he slurred, walking purposefully out of the front door and turning left towards his home.

Moira had gone through several emotions during the day. She had half expected the put-down first thing: it was, after all, quite normal for middle-aged people not to be excited about their birthdays. She certainly didn't celebrate the idea of being a year older, but she was still a bit upset about his attitude.

When she'd met Patrick Mahoney the war was on and they'd been young teenagers, drawn together by death: her dad had died at Dunkirk and Patrick's parents were far too busy with their own lives. His dad, like so many with a protected job – part-time fireman and labourer at Rolls-Royce – was busiest making money on the black market. The bombing meant easy pickings from damaged homes and, as a fireman, he was usually first in. Moira didn't know much about Patrick's mum. They lived together, but only just, and his mum spent most evenings at some servicemen's club, going home in the early hours, if at all.

One day she realised she'd missed two periods and Patrick, who was now also a volunteer fireman, said he'd stand by her and the baby. It had been an escape for both of them and weeks before David was born they got married, with one of Patrick's fireman mates as best man. A year later, and Martin came along, then Mary and three years later, Patrick junior. Joe had been born in 1951 and had turned out to be the cleverest of their kids. With five youngsters to bring up in a two-up, two-down terraced house in Normanton, life was not easy, and her Patrick was spending more and more time out with his friends.

When David was just nine the council decided that the family should not be living in a two-bedroom house with a khazi at the bottom of the garden and a tin bath, so they moved into a brand new, three-bedroom semi in Chaddesden. But Patrick's nocturnal habits did not change and Moira realised that he had expanded his father's talents for thieving and was lifting anything he could get his hands on – and that now included breaking into sheds and houses.

His first two court appearances resulted in fines that they could ill afford, but Patrick squared that by going straight back to thieving. The third time, the magistrates had had enough and would not listen to the litany of poor excuses about his upbringing and the effects of the war, and he was sent to prison for a year. Prison was the best, and worst, thing that could have happened. Moira was able to keep the family together and found the neighbours were mostly sympathetic, but Patrick used his time inside to learn some new skills, including how to get in through windows with minimum noise, and how to pick locks.

Naturally, the first prison sentence was followed by two more, until he was as proficient at professional burglary as any man could be, but he was beginning to miss his family and it was especially hard that he'd been inside for two Christmases in the Sixties, when the whole country seemed to be enjoying a boom after coming out of rationing. The "big job" he'd planned was going to be his last, he said to himself. He and two others had decided to share the proceeds, as well as the actual burglary, and drove towards Quarndon. They parked up by the church.

The first two of the three big houses they'd reccy'd were fine. Over the wrought-iron gates, round the back to the big greenhouse-type place that looked out on to the long back gardens, and then loading the ex-army kit bags with silver. The third house was a problem, and the little gang of burglars had not reckoned on two large, free-roaming Alsatian dogs. Two of the men were caught within a minute of getting over the gate, but Patrick escaped, running down the road towards Duffield, only to be caught in the glare of two headlights as the police raced to the scene.

Three years, the judge said as the three stood in the dock in Derby, and it was then that Patrick made his vow – never again. Eighteen months later and he was a free man; a month after that he was not just free, but earning good money.

He was tall, strong, and had kept himself very fit in prison, and, unlike most of the guys he knew, he'd realised that drink was a problem, and so he'd promised that he would turn over a new leaf, become a good and sober husband for the woman who'd stood by him.

David and Martin had left home as soon as they could and were now living in flats in the town centre. David was driving a dust cart and Martin was working as a decorator, both for the council. Good, steady jobs for good, steady, level-headed lads in their mid-twenties. Mary and Patrick junior had started apprenticeships: Mary at some lingerie factory in Ilkeston, and her brother with British Rail in town. They were both living at home, but working long shifts at odd hours. Patrick felt he'd managed pretty well, but in fact it was his wife who had brought each and every one up, from infancy right through to being adults.

As he reminisced, Mahoney staggered back from the Crown along the main road, back past the smelly factory, then straight on to his home. It was gone midnight when he eventually opened the door, and the house was quiet. Moira was sitting in the living room knitting, and Mahoney turned the television on, looked at the black screen and fell into his armchair. They said nothing. Moira picked up her knitting and went up to their bedroom.

Mahoney turned the television off and sat back. A tear rolled down his cheek and he put his head in his hands, remembering O'Malley's face after the crane bucket had made a big dent in his head, remembering the way his arms and legs had waved lifelessly as he tried to position the body over the shaft frame of the bridge support. Within seconds his whole body wracked as he cried and gripped his hair.

Was it going to be like this for the rest of his life, he asked himself. Make it stop, make it stop!

Five hours later he was still in his armchair. He'd slept, in stops and starts, but could not face Moira. She wouldn't understand and she must never know his horrible secret. There was no get-out clause: the Colonel was a lot thicker skinned and he never seemed bothered. In fact he'd been on holiday and had come back looking refreshed, but he also hadn't spent a lot of time on the site recently, just weekly checks and telephone conversations.

Moira came down the stairs, looked at her husband, and went into the kitchen. A few minutes later she came out with two mugs of tea, pushed one into his hands and sat down opposite him. She wanted to look into his face, but it stayed down and all she could see was the thinning crown of his head and the grey hairs that had appeared, it seemed, just this year. It looked like he was either wearing a mottled, badly coloured wig, thin on top and with sides that turned from dark to grey, or false sideburns that were blacker and bushier than the hair on his head: as black as the day she had met him.

"Something's worrying you. It's OK if you can't tell me, but you're going to have to get it out of your system. It's affecting us, the kids and probably your job," she said, leaning forward and trying to see his face.

Mahoney cradled his mug. He had no headache today, just a dull throb, and his body felt dry and grimy. This was not the time to make up: he could not face the idea of turning his mouth into a smile, giving Moira a peck and telling her everything was fine. He stayed immobile apart from taking a sip of his tea, and he felt its warmth hit his stomach – a better antidote to the depression he was feeling there could not be in the whole world.

"I'm not going to ask you about your drinking, not until you've sobered up for a few days. Why don't you go and see the doctor again?" She knew the answer to that and it went back to his upbringing. Only cissies went to doctors, boys don't cry, be a man and take it on the chin ... the list of stupid things men said when they didn't want to face human frailty, especially their own, was endless.

Mahoney took a last gulp of his tea, shuffled to his feet and went upstairs. In the bathroom he stared at a face that showed every one of his 40-plus years, and a few more. The colour was wrong. Grey was not a proper colour for skin, and his eyes, those bright sparkling headlights that had attracted the best-looking girl in Derby, seemed to have shrunk back into his head.

He threw water at his face and then filled the bowl and put soap on the flannel. Dressed only in his pants, he forced himself to wash, hard and viciously until, looking up, he saw a body that bore some resemblance to the toned muscled torso he had been so proud of. I'm forty-four and I've just thrown away my last chance of happiness and being a normal person, he thought.

Mahoney started to shake. He could not hold the razor and he knew that if he tried shaving he'd just shred his face. He sat down on the toilet seat and waited until the shaking stopped, thinking about how he would cure this latest bout. Then, clean shaven apart from one small nick, and dressed in his work clothes, he went downstairs to find that Moira had already gone and he was alone, apart from the three kids in their bedrooms, and they would not stir until both their parents had left the house.

He went to the telephone table in the hall, a piece of furniture that Moira had insisted they buy when they first installed the telephone, something the Colonel had provided and paid for when he got his first job at the farm. At the back of the drawer, hidden by the thick telephone directory, he found his prize – a half full bottle of vodka. He grabbed it, turned the cap, and took a long gulp, letting the fiery liquid course down his throat. The relief was almost instantaneous. His head cleared and he felt he could face another day. One more quick glug, and he put the bottle back, hiding it carefully.

It was a pattern that Mahoney slipped into easily. He knew he would be too drunk to drive if he was stopped, but only in the eyes of the law. He also knew that he was steadier, more relaxed and an infinitely better and more confident driver than if he'd had no drink, or was suffering from a hangover.

# 8

Joe Mahoney was a happy young man. He'd got three A-levels, in maths, geography and English, and he'd got himself a good, steady job in the Town Council Planning Department. Joe was different from the rest of his family. None of his three brothers or his sister had stayed at school for the Sixth Form, meaning none had A-levels. They were all in decent jobs, but he was looking for a higher flying career. He knew he could get a better paid job than the council, but this could lead to a proper path of growth, and he was still keen to learn.

The council seemed to be desperate to take people on, and Joe was quite happy to be given the task of filing reports and planning applications – in fact he found it interesting. He'd spent his twenty years in and around Chaddesden and had only ventured into the town centre occasionally and at weekends. The files he was reading and filing every day opened up a whole new world. Names that had just been places on a map, like Allestree, Chester Green and Alvaston, suddenly became real, with real people living there and working in businesses. It seemed that the whole of the town was in a mad rush to grow.

Rows of terraces off the Ashbourne Road were being flattened to make way for new offices and townhouses, and the old factories were finding that the same output could be achieved, not just with fewer people, but in a lot less space. So on the one hand there was contraction, but Joe was in the front line to see the new Derby grow out of the ashes of the Victorian and pre-Victorian town. Then there was the new ring road swooping along from the Pentagon Island, over the River Derwent, round the Cockpit to the west and linking up with the Uttoxeter and Ashbourne roads to the north. It was, he thought, the most exciting time to be in a new job.

He'd been interviewed by Mavis, secretary to the head of the Planning Department, John Moores, who had considered the task a bit unimportant – not demeaning, because every man, and woman, deserved to be treated with respect: that was his belief and his politics – and anyway he had meetings to attend.

Joe was expecting to be treated like a slave, as the new boy, but apart from a couple of middle-aged secretaries-cum-clerks, who spent most of the day gossiping rather than working, he was well looked after. It helped that he was young, tall, good-looking and had jet black hair, longish, but kept in place and not straggly like a hippy. It also helped that he had a smile that attracted the younger girls from almost every office in the massive building, and a plain enthusiasm about helping other people.

Joe Mahoney was a magnet for the girls, but he was at his best when he was helping the older women by moving furniture, changing light bulbs and plugging and unplugging equipment under their desks, though he wondered why they needed these things doing so frequently.

Mavis kept an eye on young Joe. On their very first meeting she had recognised that he would be a hard, dedicated worker, but possibly more importantly, his family background fitted the type of person who would get on with, and work well with, her boss, Mr Moores. He had climbed his way out of a working-class upbringing, avoiding the sweat and grime of his father's life as a quarry worker, and gained enough qualifications for an office job. Now he liked to see others try to emulate him. Joe had the makings of a "gofer" and John Moores, with his meetings, politics, social activities and growing workload, needed somebody with initiative he could trust to "go for this" and "go for that", without having to have a detailed list of exactly what was needed.

Just two months after getting the job, Joe was asked by Mavis to go to Mr Moores' office. He'd seen him around and knew he was the boss, but their paths had not really crossed.

"Come in Joe. I've heard a lot about you. Are you enjoying working in the Planning Department? Getting on with the girls OK? Finding it interesting? Mavis has told me all about you," Moores said in his deep, accent-ridden voice. Joe realised that any answers were superfluous: John Moores liked talking so he could hear his own voice.

"I understand you've been showing a lot of interest in the ring road project." Joe opened his mouth to explain that it was just one of the jobs, but Moores put a hand up. "No, that's not a criticism. I'm very pleased to see you showing an interest. We don't have any secrets in this department, do we Mavis?"

Mavis took this as her chance to smile in agreement and move back to the door. She could handle Moores when there was a problem, she could explain the details of planning applications when he was flummoxed, but she did not want to be in the same room when he was in one of his expansive, trouser belt-busting moods with his chest pumped up.

"Come and have a look at this Joe." Moores rose from his big, dark-oak desk and walked towards the back of the large, dark-oak panelled office. On a table was a four-foot-square model of part of Derby showing the new ring road in minute detail. There were even trees, and Joe could clearly see St Mary's Church and St Helen's House.

"This is what it's all about. This is the new Derby for the twenty-first century," Moores said as he flicked a switched and the street lights came on to show the model in even greater detail. "Impressed?"

Joe was open-mouthed. He'd never seen anything like it. It was as if the model builders had taken a photograph of the future and turned it into a real place. "This is fantastic Mr Moores. You must feel very proud." Joe's admiration for the model builder transferred itself to the man he had been told was almost solely responsible for turning the planners' dream into soon to be complete reality.

Moores took a pointer stick from the side of the table and waved it generally over the model. "Aye. I was always told that pride comes before a fall, but I think you can say I am proud of this." He moved the pointer from the Pentagon Island across to the new Derwent bridge. "It looks a bit complicated, but you can see how the roads will not just feed into the town centre, but also take traffic smoothly towards the Infirmary here, and then," he swung the pointer to the right, "up here to the church. That's the project that you know about, but I have plans to extend the whole scheme until we get a proper inner ring road for Derby.

"The next step will be to connect the new road at this junction," and he pointed to where the A6 turned off to the north, "right up to the Burton Road. That's going to mean a lot of demolition, mostly the old terraced houses around Abbey Street, but needs must. On the other side we'll bring the road past Babington Lane and the lower end of Normanton to link with the Burton Road – and then it will be a complete ring."

Moores put the pointer back on the side of the table and shepherded Joe to two leather couches with a low table between them. On the table were a pile of papers and folders at least a foot high, and an A3 drawing of the current project plans.

"You've made quite an impression since you joined us, and I don't just mean on the girls," Moores said as he sat down, the air escaping from the couch like a soft windy fart. "I'm told that you're a hard worker and I'm looking for someone I can trust. My problem is time. This is the biggest project Derby has ever witnessed in living memory, and it's growing, and it's that growth where the problem lies. I'm working closely with a private developer to make sure that everything is on schedule, and we're talking about millions of pounds. As well as spending time in council and Labour Party meetings, I'm also meeting the contractors and visiting the site. I've realised I can't do everything, so I would like you to be my eyes and ears on the site. I want to know about progress, any hitches, any possible problems. In effect I want to know about what's going on before it happens. I don't want full written reports. I just want someone I can totally trust to report back to me directly, and no one else."

Joe looked at the plans. In the short time he had been

at the department he had learned to decipher flat plans at a glance and turn them into real structures. He was ambitious, but he hadn't expected anything like this so soon. Not only would it get him out of the office and into a hard hat, and wearing one of those had been one of his short-term ambitions, but he would be involved in a project that had excited him since he'd first read about it in the *Telegraph*.

"Thank you Mr Moores. I won't let you down," he said.

"Right lad. The only drawback is that this may mean working some evenings and possibly a weekend or two. You're a single lad, that's one of the reasons why I'm asking you. You haven't got a wife and kids to go home to at five o'clock every night. I hope you understand."

"No, no, that's fine Mr Moores. My career is more important than a social life at the moment."

"Good. Mavis will sort everything out with the people you're working with so they don't ask questions. This is a change in role for you and if you do well we'll see about getting you a pay rise, maybe in three months or so. Let's see how you get on," Moores said as he rose from the couch, leaving an impression on the seat that would take a few minutes to return to flat, and ushered Joe out of the door.

Moores was feeling good about himself, he always did when he was able to help someone else, as long as it was good for everybody concerned. Some would call it "largesse" but he just thought back to when he had that teaching job and the other staff treated him like muck. As far as they were concerned woodwork was not a subject and they made it plainly obvious that he would not be involved in any of the academic meetings they held. That changed when he became a union officer and started to get involved in politics, but school was still a very uncomfortable and hostile environment.

No, he was well shot of teaching, and a lot better off working with the council. He had full-time officers, or experts as they liked to call themselves, but they seemed to have a different agenda. They just wanted everything to stay the same. He, meanwhile, wanted change and growth. He'd successfully forged his own path with the ring road development and made sure that, while the officers looked after the day-to-day stuff, he would head up all the important decisions. That was how he had managed to get young Joe on his personal staff, and that was why he was working so closely with Clive Browne, a real powerhouse of development and civil engineering in his opinion.

He liked Browne. Like him, Browne came from the working class and he'd done very well for himself. He had a good understanding of people and he'd got contacts in all the right places. He had been told that, as well as being invited to the House of Commons on several occasions, Browne had also been to two garden parties at Buckingham Palace.

He also delivered on his promises, and Moores liked a man whose word was his bond. If Browne said something would happen then it did. He was also generous, but in all the right ways. Moores could never, ever take a bribe and he would soon put a stop to any business relationship that involved money changing hands in brown envelopes. He knew it went on in some places, but not in his Labour Party.

That said, Browne did tend to share his good fortune

in other ways that, while not bribes, were very acceptable gifts and demonstrated his wish to work closely with the council. Meetings were often arranged in what Browne called neutral territory, perhaps at his club in Nottingham or over a long lunch or dinner somewhere that he could not have afforded to go to himself. Then there was the trip to the club in Birmingham, which, while not strictly business, was great relaxation and you had to get to know the people you were working with, didn't you?

A week or so before the planned extension to the ring road project was agreed, Browne had mentioned he had a villa in Spain and wouldn't it be a good idea to go there for a week when the contract was actually signed. Moores could see little wrong with that idea, especially as Browne had offered to send flight tickets as well as organise the chauffeur to take him to the airport. Moores had no qualms about accepting the lifts and the tickets: if Browne wanted a meeting he could decide where it was.

Moores felt that with Clive Browne he was working with the right man for the complex, multi-million pound jobs. Browne was very professional, respectful to him as a Councillor and an all-round decent guy.

Clive Browne despised John Moores. He was a fat, loud, ignorant man with no brain and even less understanding of how business worked. He was a great politician for his precious Labour Party and he had the right public persona to win over the voters of Allenton every time there was an election. He also liked to see his name and face in the local paper as much as possible.

However, he was firmly in Browne's pocket. Every

receipt for every meal had been kept, and records stored away about the trips to nightclubs and strip clubs. The week of luxury he planned at his Spanish villa would be the clincher. Dealing with a politician like Moores was different to handling the Tories, but the principle was the same.

Browne could see the town's politics swinging. A Labour government often resulted in a Tory town council, and the reaction to a national Tory government would often be the election of Labour in the town. Browne covered both sides, and his relationship with the Tory opposition was based on more straightforward methods – cash transferred direct to private bank accounts and, in the case of Matthew Palmer, a new conservatory and patio at his house in Allestree.

It had been Browne's idea to get young Joe Mahoney involved in the ring road project. His father, Patrick, had been getting progressively more unstable since the winter, and Hamilton-Pocklington was taking more and more time off with his rent boys in America and Bali. He wanted someone who would be naive and honest in reporting back, had a good understanding of what was going on at the site, and would possibly be a calming and steadying influence on Patrick Mahoney. Joe fitted those bills.

Joe Mahoney was a natural for this job. The girls in the office saw him as good-looking and friendly; the guys on the building site found him easy to get along with and eager to learn. In fact, Joe Mahoney was a sponge for knowledge. The younger labourers and apprentices had soon stopped trying it on when they found that Joe not only looked well built, but he was nobody's pushover; the older, experienced ones were flattered by his questioning and innate respect, even though he was a "bosses' boy", the son of the guy who seemed to be in day-to-day charge of the whole job, and the right-hand man of the council supremo.

The only difficulty was that, on site, nobody had first names. Everybody was either surname or nickname, and nobody was going to give either boss Mahoney or his son a nickname. Such familiarity just didn't happen, so they both became Mahoney, and the only way of working out which was which was in the context of the conversation.

# 9

PATRICK Mahoney knew something was wrong. It wasn't just the constant headaches, it was much more the fact that he was being pushed out by his family. He didn't eat at home – the crisps and a roll at the Crown were enough, and beer seemed to satisfy his appetite anyway. The doctor had told him to cut out his drinking, and he had tried, but no matter how many pints he had in the evening he still felt, not sober, but in control of his own mind, and always, always, desperately sad and missing something. He used to have a laugh with the lads, but now he just sat at the end of the bar and glowered at anyone who made any comment in his direction.

The only good thing, and it was still his little secret, was the bottle of vodka in the telephone table. Four months ago half a bottle, one of those flatter ones that fitted the drawer better, would last him a week; now he was drinking two, and sometimes three between Monday morning and Saturday. It was just a mouthful before he went to work each day, but his mouth must be getting bigger, and then it was a glass before going to bed.

But it never really stopped the shakes, just stilled them for an hour or two.

Moira had had enough. She didn't care about having no marriage any more – these things happened as you got older and middle-aged couples would go without sex for months at a time, and even then it was just a few animal thrusts and the old man would roll off and go to sleep. What was, she felt, destroying her was the constant atmosphere of fear. Patrick's days of violence and hitting out at anything, including her, had disappeared since he'd come out of prison, apart from that one slap – but in recent weeks he'd slammed the kitchen door off its hinges, he'd smashed the front garden fence when he rolled in paralytic, and the little ornaments her mum had left her were in shards in the bin. She was going to have to tackle it, and the best time was when they were alone on a Saturday afternoon – before he'd gone to the Crown.

"Patrick, I'm worried. There's something wrong and if you talk about it I might be able to help."

Mahoney put down his tea and looked over to his wife. "There's nowt wrong. I'm really sorry about that slap and it will never happen again. I promised you then, and I'm promising you now."

"Forget the slap. I have. It's just that you're different. Don't think I haven't noticed the shakes, or even the bottle of vodka in the table. I know more about you than you do yourself."

"What! Have you been checking up on me? I'm OK, I just need a drink now and again. It's OK, the doctor's going to give me some different tablets to stop the shaking and help me sleep. It's OK I tell you." Mahoney got up to attack the bottle. This was a time when he needed a drink more than ever, and since Moira knew his secret he may was well grab the vodka now.

Moira stood up and moved forward, gently pushing Mahoney back into his seat, and then knelt down by his outstretched legs. "It's OK love. We don't have secrets do we? We love each other and always have. You've always been my big man. I just want to help you be big and strong again."

Mahoney's head went down and he started to cry. Not just whimpering tears, but sobs that shook his whole torso. He clung on to his wife and the shoulder of her blouse became soaked in his tears.

"Come on love, let it out," she said holding his arm and willing all her own strength into the man who, despite it all, she loved more than anything in the world.

"I killed a man. It wasn't my fault. It was an accident, but he's dead and I did it. I can't handle it. I'm a bad bastard, I've stolen and robbed and I've paid the penalty, but I'd never really hurt anyone. Now I've killed someone. They'll hang me for it. I know they will, and it's not my fault." Mahoney's grip on his wife's arm was getting tighter and she had to move.

"Stop it. Right now. Stop it!" she shouted at him. "You've killed no one, and they don't hang people any more. You're a good man now. You're just making it up, but for God's sake I don't know why."

Mahoney felt a rush of peace and he calmly let go of Moira and sat back in the chair. His worst ever secret was out in the open now and with someone he loved and trusted.

"Just sit there love. I'll tell you everything, but nothing must ever leave this house or us two. It will be the end of everything I've tried to do since I came out of prison," Mahoney said, and he then recounted every detail of the death of O'Malley, burying the body in concrete and drowning the Land Rover in the pond at the farm.

"I'm going to make us another pot of tea and have a think. You just sit there and relax. You're still my man and this accident changes nothing," Moira said after a short silence when Mahoney had finished the story.

Patrick was a big useless lump in a crisis, like every man she knew. This needed a strong woman with a logical brain, and she was the right woman for the job, Moira thought to herself as she filled the pot, pouring boiling water on to the tea leaves. She walked back into the living room, put the pot down, and went across to her husband, cradling his head in her arms.

"It's OK. Nobody is going to hurt any of us. Nobody needs to know anything. You've told me, so there's no need to bottle it up any more, but if you do want to talk about it then tell me, nobody else. It's not your secret any more, it's our secret and that's a big difference."

Mahoney nodded, and in a small voice she had not heard for nearly thirty years he mumbled agreement and promised never to tell another soul.

It was two days later that Moira decided to put a cork firmly on this particular bottle, and realised that she needed to confront the real villain: Colonel Hamilton-Pocklington, the dirty little homo.

"Good morning Moira. What was so urgent that you needed to come and see me here?" the Colonel greeted Moira. She'd got the bus and walked to the Manor hoping she wouldn't be seen, certainly not by anyone who recognised her. It had been a long walk on a hot summer morning, and she was grateful for the cool of the big hall at the Manor.

The Colonel was also pleased to see her. He'd been hearing some disturbing things about her husband on the ring road site and was not very keen to speak to him direct. Perhaps his rather mousey little wife could get the message across? She'd been discreet after finding him "in flagrante" so to speak, and kept her side of the bargain. In fact, giving Mahoney gainful employment when he came out of prison had proved to be a good move all round.

"Come into the drawing room. The help has gone shopping so I have had to make tea myself, I hope that's OK," he said, smiling.

You creepy, oily, sanctimonious, little boy-loving poofter, Moira thought as she returned his smile and allowed him to usher her into the drawing room. "That will be lovely," she said. "I just wanted to get a few things clear about my Patrick."

She sat opposite the Colonel and, being a mother and a woman, poured tea for both of them, adding two sugars to the Colonel's after he'd responded to her questioning look with two fingers.

"I think we should cut out the niceties and get down to the reason why I'm here," Moira said. She wanted this over with as quickly as possible. She had no real problem with the Colonel's homosexuality – it disgusted her, and he did as well, but simply being queer was, in itself, not a crime in her opinion. It was that combined with his personality and the facts she had learnt from her husband that really made her despise him.

"I know about O'Malley. I know everything about it, and what you made my husband do was despicable and more horrible than anything I could imagine in my worst nightmares."

The Colonel sat back, and opened his mouth, but no words came out. What could he say? He wanted to end this conversation with a heavy, blunt instrument – like the big brass andiron by the fire – but he knew instinctively that was not an option. "What do you want? Why are you telling me this?"

"I'm telling you because you need to know that I also know all about you. You know I saw you with that young boy last year, and now I know that you are, to all intents and purposes, a murderer, or at the very least an accessory to a vicious killing. What I want, we can talk about." Moira was feeling in complete control. She'd got the Colonel by the balls – a concept that filled her with disgust, as would any physical contact with this rich slime-ball.

"You can't do anything. I didn't kill O'Malley, your precious husband did. If I'm accused, he goes down for a long, long time – and you will be left with nothing." The Colonel spat out the words.

Moira let a small smile creep on to her face. She'd anticipated his reaction and knew it was bluff.

"You will tell nobody. You'll do anything to save your precious skin." Moira enjoyed using the word in a derogatory way, just as the Colonel had spoken about her Patrick. "To you, we are nothing, but our silence is all that's keeping you from an end to all this," and Moira waved her right arm to indicate the whole of Morley Manor. "No more trips around the world; no more fine wines; no more plush dinners; but lots and lots of little boys in prison, and some very big boys as well, so I'm led to believe," she added, centring her smile on his now pale pallor.

"I think we need some compensation for everything you've done. This has damaged my family and hurt me. Forget Patrick, he's just your employee, but both he and I know enough to put you inside prison for many years."

The Colonel nursed his teacup and wished he'd had something a lot stronger. This unpleasant woman was right, of course, and silence must be maintained at all costs.

"What do you want? You realise this is blackmail, so you'll be going to prison as well if it ever gets out, and I don't think your kids would ever want to see their jailbird mum again," the Colonel said, desperately trying to claw back the initiative.

Moira steeled herself for the crunch. She'd given this some thought, but was afraid that she would collapse if the Colonel refused or, worse, wanted to negotiate.

"I just think we deserve some compensation. Patrick has told me how much you're making and it's a lot more than we will ever see in our lives. I think we deserve a small share, especially as Patrick has done a lot more than just work for you.

"I don't want a lot, and I don't want a big lump sum straight off. That would look suspicious. What I want from you is £200 going into this bank account," and she passed the Colonel a slip of paper, "every month. But it mustn't come direct from you. You can put it through Derwent Bank or one of your other companies, but I want it to look above board as an honest, regular gift so we don't get stung for tax."

The Colonel looked at the slip of paper and the carefully written out Midland Bank account number. He needed time. This was the second time in a few months that he had been handed an ultimatum and he knew he was not smart enough to knock Moira down in price, and anyway, this was not a massive amount in the nature of things. All he had to do was invent a couple of new employees and work the salary through to Moira's account. What was even better was that she had not asked for a thousand pounds or more straight up. With regular payments he could stay in control of the situation and keep close tabs on Mahoney at work.

"For a woman you're a hard businessman," the Colonel said. "You know I can afford this and you've pitched your dirty blackmail demand at a level that means I lose a little for a long time, but right now you have the ammunition. I want you to get out of my house and never come back. The money will be paid, but remember that I have friends who could remove you and that husband of yours off the face of the earth painfully, slowly, and quietly, so I demand absolute silence from you both."

He stood up and motioned for Moira to leave the room. She was about to ask for a lift to the bus stop in Morley, but thought it best to leave quietly while she was winning. As he shut the door behind her, she allowed herself a self-satisfied smile. That, she thought, went exactly to plan – and a lot better than it could have done.

The Colonel went back into the drawing room and took out a small glass tumbler from the cabinet. A ten-year-old Aberlour would do the trick this early in the day: dry, not peaty, but with a mellowness that stroked rather than attacked his taste buds. People, well other people, simply do not appreciate the finer things in life, he thought. He took a small sip of the single malt whisky, savouring the flavour on his lips and tongue, and then a large glug. It seemed to hit his stomach, by-passing his mouth and throat.

He would have to keep a close eye on the Mahoney family. The wife, while she was a vicious blackmailer, had devised a good plan: not enough to hurt his bank balance, but enough to top up her salary. He wondered if she planned to use the extra cash to escape those kids and that small house in a poor area of a duff suburb.

# 10

CLIVE Browne was seeing his plans come to fruition. From hard labour on the railways straight after the war, he'd built up a business with a profile just under the immediate radar. His success was based on a simple premise and a nose for a good deal. He would know instinctively what development projects would generate short- and long-term profits and he would invest borrowed money. He could always do better than the bank rate even if it meant going abroad and keeping his financial dealings very private. This meant that he was able to offer developers and contractors money up front in the right quantity to cover their liabilities.

The combination was to appeal to their greed, by metaphorically waving seven-figure sums of cash in front of their eyes, and show them that the return on the development would be well over the borrowing interest rate. The result was that the development took place as expected, and promised by the developer, and Clive was able to take his percentage, not from the initial loan, but from the price paid by the eventual buyer.

The only downside was that he had to keep a lot of balls in the air at once and make sure that developers and builders stuck rigidly to their part of the bargain, and that included quality, timekeeping and budgets. Clive Browne discovered that having big people – physically big, not mentally – working for him as enforcers meant he could instil the right behaviour amongst his debtors. He could not tolerate weak links in his chains of business and his enforcers were able to keep projects in line, often by just turning up and asking to see the progress reports.

Derwent Bank Construction was one of the current jewels in his crown. The Colonel was rarely in this country and when he was it was just to attend posh county functions in Derbyshire and Nottinghamshire, to which Clive invariably received an invitation. He had been dealing with new money for most of his business life, so it was good to be in contact with old money and a potentially new revenue stream.

The call from the Colonel had not been expected and he did not want a meeting, but the man wanted to talk and said it couldn't be over the telephone. He settled on four days' time, with the weekend in the middle, not for any particular reason, but to give the impression he was too busy until then, and to let the Colonel know that he was not a priority. In fact, he was a lot keener to spend time inspecting potential new development sites and his new hobby, stocking the 160-acre farm in Leicestershire with prime cattle. He'd bought the farm because his wife and daughters wanted somewhere to give their horses more freedom and space, and also because it was close to East Midlands Airport and connections to Heathrow on the twin-engined Short aircraft he called the flying shoebox.

Sandra looked up from her desk as the receptionist held the door open for Tim Hamilton-Pocklington. "Colonel, what a pleasure to see you again," she said, smiling and shaking hands professionally but impersonally and firmly. "Mr Browne is just on a call at the moment, but please take a seat. Can I get you a tea or coffee, or will Mr Browne be offering you something a little stronger?" she asked, with the same smile covering up her disgust for a man she thought of as despicable, despite the fact that he was landed gentry.

"Thank you," the Colonel replied, seeing in Sandra the same powerful traits as his sister, and thinking that some women were just too clever for their own good. He moved over to the rich Italian leather settee, which looked expensive, but he knew that the upholstery had been adjusted so that he would sink deep into its luxury. He also knew that getting out again could not be done with dignity and he'd have to struggle, pulling himself up on the armrest. It was another subtle trick that Clive Browne used to put others off their stride and start every meeting with him being the dominant character. The only way to overcome this was to stand instead of sit, but he didn't know how long Browne was going to be.

Sandra was still standing waiting for a response to her question about whether he wanted a tea or coffee.

"No, that's fine. I'll wait until I see Mr Browne, but thank you very much for asking," the Colonel replied, knowing that, while he was desperate for a coffee, and Sandra was renowned for the quality of the Italian coffee she made, he would look even more silly struggling to get out of the settee without spilling a hot drink in a cup and saucer.

Clive Browne was not on the phone, he was flicking through some plans for a proposed development on railway land at Toton. He was also keeping an eye on what was happening in Sandra's office through the two-way mirror. Visitors' behaviour allowed him the opportunity to get all his thoughts in order, while they had their discomfort maximised. Five minutes should be OK for the Colonel: enough to get him settled, but not too comfortable, and then making the most of the settee's low upholstery as he wriggled upright.

"Tim, such a pleasure to see you. Come in, come in." Browne had opened the office door and taken a step out, waving his arm back to invite the Colonel in.

He followed the Colonel in, waved towards two eminently more comfortable armchairs, both in the same deep red leather as the settee in Sandra's office, and walked over to the well-stocked drinks cabinet. "I'm sure you'd like a drink after negotiating the A52 to get here. Whisky?" Browne asked, knowing that the Colonel would not refuse.

"That would be great." Browne selected a large, short cut-glass tumbler and took a clear glass bottle of golden Balvenie single malt from the back of the shelf. He couldn't stand the stuff himself: while he was not a teetotaller, he only drank fine wines and then when he was socialising. Alcohol was fine, but never mix it with business, was one of his maxims.

The Colonel savoured his drink, wishing that the bottle was nearer, but knowing that his glass would not be refilled unless he asked, and he was not going to do that. Browne may be a connoisseur of fine wines, and obviously whisky, but there were times when quantity was better than quality, he thought.

"I'll come straight to the point," he said, looking over the top of his glass. "We have a problem and I need your advice. I'm being blackmailed and if it comes out it's going to affect our partnership."

Browne sat back, rested his elbows on the side of the armchair and steepled his fingers. "I think you'd better tell me the facts. I don't want the sanitised facts or those that make you look good. I know enough about you and your predilections to have you put away anyway, so I want the truth, and you know I can tell if you are trying to pull a flanker."

The Colonel, initially taken aback that Browne knew all about his taste for young boys, realised that he had nowhere to hide. If he was to get out of this mess then Browne was the only one who could help. He sat back and told the full story, from giving Mahoney the job on the farm and then the ring road site, through O'Malley's accidental death, to the blackmail by Moira Mahoney. The only thing he missed out was the reason for meeting O'Malley at the site. He didn't want Browne to think he was cheating him.

Browne had not moved. He'd taken in every word the Colonel said and felt confident that he was not telling any lies, embellishing the truth, or hiding important parts of the story.

"You really are a fool aren't you? Just one question: what were you and O'Malley rowing about? He would never have been my choice of aggregates supplier. I always go direct, not through middle men."

"He was trying to rip me off and push the prices up. It happened soon after you and I had agreed the partnership and there was no way I was going to allow some jumped-up supplier to control the job."

Browne knew what had to be done, but he was not going to share the solution with this weak-livered individual. As far as he was concerned, Hamilton-Pocklington had caused the whole debacle and any further involvement, certainly in putting things right, would just increase the risk of disaster. So far he could deny this meeting ever took place. There was no record of it, apart from the remarkable memory of Sandra – and she was the only person in the world he trusted implicitly.

"Tim, you will leave here now and as far as I am concerned you have never been here. You are incapable of carrying out simple tasks like heading up Derwent Bank, but that's something we will leave for another day. You will continue to employ Mahoney and act as if nothing has happened and he certainly must never know that I have an interest, and you will continue to pay his wife.

"Most importantly, you and I will never speak again until I contact you, probably through a third party. Is that all clear?" Browne did not want a reply, just a response, and the Colonel gave him what he needed.

"Yes, of course Clive. I'll leave everything in your hands," he said as he got out of the chair and headed towards the door that Browne had opened. They said no more, but Sandra still gave him that power smile as she wished him a safe drive back.

She then turned the speaker from Browne's office off as he came through.

"You heard all that?" he asked her. "Obviously no notes and scrub any reference to the meeting off all diaries. And you'd better get hold of Marcus and Shaun. I'll need to see them sometime tomorrow."

The problem is not Mrs Mahoney, he thought, it's her husband. If he can be silenced then the blackmail can stop. She wouldn't dare go to the police about the O'Malley business, and if she did it would be quick and simple to ensure Mahoney took all the blame.

The Colonel was petrified and he had him so tightly by the balls that he almost owned him, lock, stock and barrel. No, get rid of the threat of Mahoney opening his mouth and the problem would be permanently solved.

The next day he briefed his two top enforcers on exactly what had to be done, quietly and quickly. He also explained to these ex-professional wrestlers that this was not a job for suits and ties; they needed to blend into the background of a building site that on a Sunday was almost deserted.

Marcus and Shaun had, in their eyes, always stayed legal, but they knew that summary justice solved most problems. After two years as bouncers in Sheffield, working for a number of clubs, life had got a little warm and they'd decamped to Nottingham. The problem in Sheffield was that they both found it difficult to move with the times. A group of lads having had a beer too many would find they were ejected from the club and, if they decided to argue – and beer would always raise the macho temperature – Shaun and Marcus would select the ringleader of the group and give him a slap or two. They never came back.

The difficulty arose because they treated all punters the same and the club owners began to get nervous. There were certain families in the city, and not those who were simply blood relatives, who needed to be treated with more respect – extreme respect in some cases. Marcus and Shaun were very good at keeping order and taking control, but not so good at differentiating who was a VIP punter and who was just out for a good time. When they discovered a couple of lads who had set up shop in the gents they took swift action. Both the drug dealers lost their money, which was later stuffed into a charity box; lost their stash of marijuana and ready-rolled joints, flushed down the loos and dropped into a drain; and they both ended up in hospital with broken fingers – and a message ringing in their ears about not being able to roll joints or count money for a while.

Unfortunately these lads were a well-connected sales outlet for an enterprise that also offered protection and loans. It was also an organisation that was controlled by important customers for clubs all round Sheffield.

Clive Browne recognised the talents of Marcus and Shaun and knew they would provide the type of total, silent loyalty he demanded. He also knew that they would only do what they were told, no more and no less. Initiative was not a word either understood. They also came from Finland or north-west Russia and had all the traits of northern Scandinavians, including a good understanding of English, a very white complexion, and the build, height and strength that would intimidate most humans. These two were also, it seemed, without empathy: they simply had no feelings for the people they were disciplining.

Shaun made the call to the Derwent Bank site office in Derby. "Can I speak to Mr Mahoney please?"

"That's me," Joe Mahoney replied, unfazed that the phone should ring on a Sunday when he was the only man on site. His brow furrowed as he tried to work out an accent he had not heard before. "How can I help?"

"I've been asked to come and see you about a problem with the cement you are using. We have been told that it is taking too long to set and it may cause a delay in other work," Shaun said.

To Joe this was new, but not too surprising. With so many different aspects of the project on the go at the same time, it was critical that each element synchronised with others. The Japanese had a phrase for it, Just In Time, but so far the concept had not travelled to the UK. He also knew that his father was not on site and, given his increased drinking, he could not be sure when he would be. In any case, he could kill two birds with one stone here and report to Mr Moores and his dad after the meeting. His boss would definitely be happy that he had used his initiative, and he hoped his father would understand why it was good for him as well.

"Fine. When would you like to come over?" he replied to Shaun, still wondering where that accent came from.

"About seven o'clock tonight would be best. We know where you are," Shaun said, hoping that the Mahoney guy would agree as they wanted to get this job out of the way as soon as possible.

"Yes. I'll be here. I'll put the kettle on," Joe replied in his usual friendly voice. The line went dead, even though he was happy to have a brief chat and anyway, he thought, it would have been polite to confirm the time. Still, he'd got enough work to do going through the amended plans his department had received for the extension, even though it was a Sunday afternoon and he'd only dropped in to check some files while it was quiet and the workforce was away.

Marcus and Shaun drove down the A52 in a nondescript white van. It was as near anonymous as any vehicle could be and fitted well with their uniform of dirty and scuffed denim dungarees over grey-white shirts.

Joe opened the door to the office to let his visitors in,

but his welcoming smile vanished instantly as Shaun slammed him from one side of the office to the other, and Marcus took up position in front of the now closed door. There was no escape.

"You Mahoney?" Shaun asked as he grabbed hold of Joe by his left arm.

"Yes. Who the hell are you?" he replied, before a back-handed swipe from Shaun's left hand smacked into his mouth, dislodging teeth and leaving a bloody smear across his face. There was no reply as Shaun, still holding Joe's left arm, straightened it and then slammed the elbow firmly and fast across the high back of the heavy wooden chair. The snap of bone was followed by an anguished scream, cut short after less than a second by Shaun's hand clamped across his mouth.

Joe was in shock more than pain. He knew his arm was broken, he knew he'd lost some teeth, but he simply didn't know why and these guys were not going to tell him.

Leaving his position guarding the door, Marcus moved forward to deliver his favourite punch. He hit Joe right between the eyes at the top of the nose, not just breaking his nose almost beyond repair, but knocking him unconscious. The blow also took Joe off his feet and he spun round, falling on to the cast-iron stove, striking his head on the corner, and sinking to the ground. He didn't move.

"He's dead. We've killed him," Shaun said after he'd knelt down and checked Joe's pulse. "Let's clear up here and get him into the van. You wipe that stove down. We can't leave any marks anywhere."

Marcus took a rag from the sink and soaked it in water to clean the stove, while Shaun pulled Joe's lifeless body into the middle of the office. Neither noticed the door handle turn, but both heard the creak of the door as Patrick Mahoney walked into his office.

"Who are you?" Marcus said as he grabbed hold of Patrick.

Mahoney would have fought back, but the beer he'd had meant that, yet again, he was slow and heavy and he couldn't think straight. He'd only come back from the pub to pick up his van, and now he was faced with two massive bears of guys and there, on the floor, was his son, not moving and looking unconscious.

"Joe!" he cried as he fell forward, trying to kneel down. "What have you done to my son?"

This was not in the script that Browne had given them. He'd never said there'd be two Mahoneys. Marcus spun the older man round, rammed the cloth he'd been using to clean the stove into his mouth, and slammed him into the chair.

"Tie him up and secure that gag in his mouth," Shaun said, reverting to Finnish, a language that Mahoney thought sound like a collection of vowels and guttural whoops. "I need to use the phone to find out what he wants us to do."

Shaun moved towards the desk and, with his back to both men and the body, took the telephone and dialled the number that had been sworn to secrecy.

"It's Shaun," he said as the phone was picked up and a murmured grunt was given in reply. "We've got a problem. We've silenced the one called Mahoney, and that's permanent, but another guy with the same name, an older one, has walked in. Do you want us to finish the job?"

"No," Browne said quickly: he disliked physical violence and certainly did not want to be associated with more dead bodies, even though they were sometimes necessary. He had to think fast, but that was what he was good at.

"Get the body and Mahoney into your van and make sure he's secure and quiet. You know the lock-up by the canal and river in Shardlow? Meet me there in two hours. In the meantime make sure that the office you are in has absolutely no trace of your visit.

"When you get to the lock-up, get it set up for an interview. You know what I mean. I'll be there in two hours, make sure it's set up."

Shaun put the phone down and, in Finnish, explained to Marcus what was to be done.

# 11

CLIVE Browne was deep in thought as he drove along the A453. Mahoney was still the major problem, but he was adamant about not wanting any more deaths. He knew enough about Mahoney, but Mahoney knew nothing about him. That was part of the deal with Derwent Bank. His role was purely financial, a one-way investment, and Derwent Bank would head up all the public aspects. If the Colonel and his employees were going to become a liability, and right now that seemed very likely, perhaps it was time to cut and run. He may not have been lily white during his business career, but reputation mattered and he was not going to be tainted by others' stupidity and criminal activities, certainly as so far that involved two dead bodies, and an unsolved problem.

He'd chosen the Shardlow lock-up well. It was away from any residential areas and secluded, but it was also well known that boat repairers often worked odd hours, so lights and the sound of the generator would not be noticed. As an added precaution he parked the old grey Hillman two streets away where it joined several others and did not stand out.

Marcus and Shaun had got to the lock-up well within the two hours and had the generator working. They left the body in the van and half walked, half dragged the older Mahoney in, sitting him in a chair at the far end and tying his arms and legs to it. The gag was still in place, but they'd loosened it because he seemed to be having some difficulty breathing.

As Browne entered through the small door in the side, Shaun flicked the switch and three powerful spotlights centred on Mahoney in his chair. Before, he'd been able to see a bare room with white-washed brick walls, with the end wall comprising two large wooden doors. Now he could see nothing and was unable to turn his head away from the lights that were not just blinding him, but were so intense that, even if he shut his eyes the pain of the light seared through into his brain.

"The wages of sin are death," Browne said, using a tone of voice and phraseology that Mahoney would remember, but would not be recognised as anything Browne would say normally, "and you have been very, very sinful.

"It's unfortunate that your son is lying dead, but you know it's your fault don't you? If you hadn't screwed up, then none of this would have happened. Unfortunately for all of us, while you have got us into this mess, you are also the person who is going to get us out.

"You are nothing to me. I could crush you like an annoying wasp, but I'm going to give you one last chance to redeem yourself, keep your life and prevent your dear wife from going to prison, not just as a dirty little blackmailer, but an accessory to a murder you committed."

Mahoney had no idea who this person was. He'd never heard the voice before, but he seemed to know everything. It wasn't the Colonel, that he was sure of, and these two animals seemed to be in awe of him.

"Your son has had an accident. He was in the wrong

place at the wrong time. His death is your responsibility, so you are going to dispose of his body – and that's something you are well versed in anyway – and make it all look like an accident," Browne said. He then explained to Mahoney and his captors exactly what was going to happen.

He knew that Mahoney had been a half decent burglar of commercial properties, but a pathetic failure as a house breaker, so he would make use of those skills as well as his physical strength. As a precaution, and to make sure he toed the line, he would also use the experience and talents of his two enforcers.

He nodded to Marcus and Shaun and walked back out of the side door. Leaving the lock-up, Browne retraced his steps to the car and then drove a different route home, heading south along the M1 and cutting across round Loughborough to the A46, disappearing into the quiet country lanes around Wartnaby. If the car was seen it would never be remembered or identified.

Mahoney was in no position to argue. That disembodied voice had come up with a solution that meant life, or what was left of it, could carry on and none of this would affect his wife, daughter or the three remaining boys. If he'd had a choice and had thought about it he'd probably have done it this way anyway, he thought – but he had no choice. All the options were bound up in the complex situation he found himself in and the deep understanding that he was a killer and he would now have to deal with his own son's body. While it was in his hands, it was also out of them.

When the well-spoken man had left, the blazing spotlight was extinguished. Instead of seeing nothing in the unrelenting glare Mahoney could now see nothing in the blackness. Gradually his eyes adjusted and for what seemed hours he was alone, bound to a chair and unable to move, and knowing that the dead body of his son was just feet away.

He began to feel tired and then there was a clatter as a door opened, a light was switched on and the two thugs reappeared. They took hold of Joe's body and carried it to the van and returned to untie Patrick.

Shaun drove the van into Derby, checked there were no other cars or bobbies on their beat, and snuck into an alleyway off East Street, killing the lights and effectively hiding the vehicle in plain sight. He opened the rear doors and Mahoney got out, watched carefully by Shaun as Marcus pulled the body out and hoisted it up on to his shoulder. Mahoney carried the short ladder as the pair walked round to the side entrance of Boots, while Shaun stayed neared the van, hidden among dustbins.

Mahoney's long-unused skills came flooding back as he positioned the ladder against the wall and climbed up. On the roof he knew just where to tread without breaking through a potentially fragile ceiling. Marcus carried Joe as if he was just a child's toy, not a dead weight, and followed in Mahoney's booted footsteps as they climbed up the roof, stopping just before its apex next to a skylight, some forty feet off the ground. Looking down there was a steeply inclined roof, then an old gutter and then a vertical drop into another alley. He and Mahoney placed the body with the feet facing the drop and arms outstretched and let it go.

The body of Joe Mahoney slid smoothly down the roof tiles and his feet went over the gutter, but his jacket sleeve caught and his whole body was held, almost in mid-air, until the dead weight snapped the gutter and the body dropped on to the stone flags below.

His father reached up and snapped the lock of the skylight on the roof, and started to move back the way he had come, but Marcus stopped him.

"You go over the roof. Come down another way. Leave no trace," the big Finnish bear said.

Mahoney nodded and moved up and over the roof apex. He understood that break-ins like this were usually the work of two people and there had been two sets of footprints leading to where they were, so there had to be only one set on the way back.

Ten minutes later, all three were back in the white van as Shaun manoeuvred on to Uttoxeter New Road and skirted the town to drop into Spondon, letting a badly shaken Mahoney walk the remaining mile home. He would not talk to anybody: in fact, he might have been struck dumb by the evening's events.


Moira had gone to bed by the time he got in. For the first time in months he was sober and late home, in fact, stone cold sober and at 4am. Moira would be grilling him again, he thought, and this time he could not say anything. The two animals had made it clear that they knew his family and knew where he lived. They would not hesitate to take action against him, or worse, his wife and kids, but the guy who really frightened him was the faceless voice. Not only did he seemingly know everything, but he sounded cold, hard, and without any emotion.

He'd met guys like that in prison, usually on their way from high security to an open prison and then licence: psychopathic he thought they'd been called. Whatever name you gave them, they were devious and only seemed to smile when someone was having pain inflicted on them. There was no need to be afraid of the nonces in prison, but you never wanted to get on the bad side of one of those psychopathic guys.

Mahoney made himself a cup of tea and went into the living room. Sitting in his armchair meant he would not be disturbed by Moira when she eventually got up, and it gave him time to think of his story. The faceless voice had told him what to say: now all he had to do was remember it.

"Where were you last night?" Moira asked as she came into the living room. She looked closer at her husband and knew something was wrong, badly wrong. "What's the matter? Has something happened?"

"I've had the police out. Joe has been found dead in an alley off St Peter's Street," he said.

"Oh my god! Why didn't you wake me? It's my son!"

"I told them I'd tell you, and there was no woman police officer with them. They'll be coming back in a few minutes they said." Moira was confused. She didn't understand, but she wanted to know what had happened anyway.

"Are you sure it's Joe? What happened? He wasn't working this weekend. What was he doing in town? Where is he?" Moira's questions fell out one after the other, leaving no time for a reply. She knew the Colonel had to be involved and that was her first plan. Screw that bastard to a wall and remove those bodily items he felt closest to. Her son's death and the Colonel had to be connected. Joe was a good lad: he would not be getting involved in anything wrong.

Mahoney slowly and carefully told Moira the story, or

at least the story he said he'd been given by the police. The police would be round soon enough, but he'd overcome that problem when it arrived. The first job was for him to persuade Moira to take care of Mary and Patrick junior, who would still be in their beds, and then get the message to David and Martin. That would keep her busy while he handled the police visit, which should be within the next few minutes.

"I'll look after Patrick and Mary, you stay here and answer the police questions when they turn up," Moira said, echoing his thoughts.

It was exactly as the faceless voice had said. A police constable and a woman police constable came to the door minutes later. Moira was upstairs as he faked surprise. It was not difficult. He was still stunned from the night before.

Moira and the two children came downstairs.

"You need to tell the boys. Take these two with you," Patrick said and ushered all three to the front door.

The WPC, dreading the job of looking after the bereaved, was not going to stand in their way. This Mahoney guy seems to have got it all in hand, she thought. Any questions she had did not need the mother or the rest of the family so, when the three had left, she made the tea, as was conventional in such circumstances, and joined her colleague to ask about Joe – when he was last seen, where he had been, who his friends were.

Mahoney was happy to tell them the truth – up to a point – and stressed that Joe was a good, solid working lad and had never been in trouble, but the police persisted in sticking to this story about Joe being involved in a burglary that went wrong. One of the things Mahoney had learned from his brushes with the law was that once the plods had an idea they would not budge. In this case, no matter how much he told them his son was straight, they were going to believe their own story, and he was not about to disabuse them by recounting the real facts.

Mahoney and Moira were picked up that afternoon. The police took them to Derbyshire Royal Infirmary where they together identified the body of their son. DI Ludden, who'd been handed the case that morning when he got in, found both parents very quiet and withdrawn. He didn't expect wailing and gnashing of teeth, but the family usually demonstrated deeper emotion than the few tears from the mother and stoicism from the father. Not his concern, he thought. He'd wrap the case up in a few hours, or at least as soon as the post mortem result came through.

Mahoney rang the Colonel and gave him the version that the faceless voice had told him, the same as he'd told the police, and explained that his van was still at the ring road site.

# 12

---

Simon Jardine was knackered. He'd been covering Crown Court all week and also trying to wheedle interesting stories out of council committees. At the forefront of his mind had been the forthcoming meeting with Councillor Moores. Mavis, Councillor Moores' PA, had called to postpone the interview, but she had made it plain it was a postponement, not a cancellation.

Crown Court would have to take precedence and he was, after all, a junior reporter who had to prove his skills in writing all sorts of news. The case was a sex assault charge and the middle-aged woman victim had been put through the wringer by the defence. With so many salacious details being aired, halfway through the week he was expecting a bit of light relief. In fact all his juvenile thoughts vanished within seconds of the woman taking the stand, and, after he'd decided the brute was guilty, he lost interest and just got on with reporting those facts that a family newspaper could print, and there were not many.

What the case did do was give him to time to think about the Joe Mahoney investigation that Dave Green had got him into. He had to admit that hearing about Tom's past and his current sideline as a private dick had been a bit of a surprise. Ah well, you just never knew with some folks, he thought.

Life was beginning to get back to normal and he'd put the Mahoney business on the back burner. Two things helped. First was the visit of Chicken Shack to Derby. They were a great little rock band that he'd first heard at university last year and been impressed with the singer Christine Perfect. She'd left the band and he'd seen them within a few weeks of starting work as a reporter in Derby, his first ever music review in fact, and now they were back in town for a second gig. They remembered him and it had been a great evening, ending with far too many beers at the Cat after the band had finished their set.

Then there was the short holiday at home for his dad's birthday. This had been an excuse to detox from his alcohol diet for a day or two and get some good home cooking inside him. It was also a chance to get his washing done without having to traipse down to the launderette. All a bit like university really, he thought. He spent two days walking the family spaniel, Bruce, and generally being a loving and dutiful son, but three days at home was enough and on Tuesday he called Dave Green and set up a meeting at the Exeter Arms early that evening.

Dave was already there as Simon walked in straight from the station.

"I've had a nod from the Coroner's office. The post mortem shows that young Joe didn't die in that alleyway and that makes it murder or at the very least an unexplained death," Dave said. "Ludden is royally pissed off. He's in charge of the case, and instead of tying it all up as a misadventure in a day, he's now got to open a full investigation. His problem is that he's got no leads, nothing to go on at all."

As Simon absorbed this piece of news – well, it wasn't news really because both he and Dave knew that Joe Mahoney had not been involved in the burglary, that was too far-fetched – the door swung open and Tom Freeman walked in and ordered a large Coke.

"Well the three musketeers are here again," he said, drawing up a stool and joining Dave and Simon in the window bay.

"Hi Tom. What's the word on the street then?" Dave asked.

"Nothing so far. It's a bit of a mystery, and the IQ of our much-loved police force is not going to get them very far," Tom answered. "The problem is that not only do they have no cast-iron leads, but there was no burglary. Nothing was stolen and the break-in was just that. Somebody broke in through the skylight, but never went into the store. The police are totally flummoxed and you can see why. A few days ago they had the cut-and-dried accidental death of a toerag trying to break into a shop; today they have the dead body of a completely innocent young man who was found somewhere he didn't die.

"None of the usual criminal fraternity know anything about it. As far as they're concerned, Joe had never been in trouble and his father, Patrick, seems to have completely turned away from his old criminal past and been straight ever since he got out of Nottingham Prison. His old mates say they've never been in contact with him."

Dave nodded, acknowledging Tom's information and then, bringing Simon into the conversation, said: "I can understand the police frustration. It's a known fact that if this is a murder, or even manslaughter, then the chances are that it was either carried out by a family member or by someone known to the victim."

"The police have trawled all those and got nowhere," Tom said.

"Yes. I've just given you the likely scenario based on statistics, but this definitely seems to defy logic. I want to know what happened. I owe it to Moira and it's gnawing at me. The collective brains and nous around this table is better than a station full of coppers, so we should be able to come up with a way forward," Dave added.

Simon, along with the other two, stared into his drink, absorbing Dave's back-handed praise and trying to put into words a possible link that even he felt was too outlandish to suggest.

"I'm not saying that it means anything, and you two are much better qualified than me, but should we look at the connection between father and son? The ring road project seems to be the only link. Joe was working with the Planning Department and his father was foreman at the site, and his father is the only one we know to have a fairly recent criminal link. I mean the business over the paint at the Allenton farm," he said, and sat back expecting to be put down by the more experienced pair he was talking to.

"That's not quite as daft as you might think," Dave said immediately. "I've had a call from Moira Mahoney and she wants to see me. There's no way it's an invite to get inside her knickers again – that was a long time ago and she's not going to stray from hubby again – so it will be interesting to hear what she says.

"Simon. You sniff around the Planning Department people, but be discreet. I don't want any of this getting back to Newsdesk and, if it does lead somewhere, I don't want a visit from the plods or any of those big-booted construction workers. Has your interview with Councillor Moores been rearranged yet?" Dave added, trying to make it sound a little light-hearted. He carried on without waiting for Simon's reply. "Tom. Can you cover our backs? If word gets out that we're sniffing around and asking questions, either from the police or the less savoury types you know, I would much rather this was seen as a bit of investigative newspaper reporting than amateur sleuthing."

Tom nodded and, sensing that his private detective input into the meeting was over, said to Simon: "There's a party at Paul Ruthin's place – well, actually, the back room at the Cat – on Thursday. Do you want to come along? I'm sure he'd be pleased to see you."

Paul's parties generally wavered between mind-numbingly boring and outrageous festivals of queerdom with all the colour and leather that entailed. Simon and Tom had always been able to handle the festivities, if not the boring parties. Neither was gay and they were quite comfortable in their sexuality. They did not feel intimidated by homosexuals and often found the conversation stimulating and interesting, especially when it got round to artistic matters and music. It was also a pleasant change for Tom to have a conversation with people who were not trying to get into his bed – one of the problems of being a good-looking, personable DJ.

"Yeah, that sounds OK. Are you working?" Simon asked.

"Yes. At Tiffanys, but they have a big band night so I'll be able to stop by about 11.30 and I'll leave it to the Miller Band to finish the evening off. I'll come round afterwards," Tom said as all three got up. Tom's car was outside and Dave and Simon walked off back to the *Telegraph.*

Dave Green dialled Moira's number hoping she'd pick up. If either of the children did, he was ready with an innocuous, "Is that Mr or Mrs Jones?"; if Patrick picked up then it was a bit more difficult. He could easily get away with the wrong number bit, but it meant that he was at home and not at work, and that did not augur well for a meeting with Moira.

"Hello, Mrs Mahoney. Can I help you?"

First hurdle jumped successfully. "Moira. It's me, Dave. You wanted to see me?"

"Dave, thank god you called." Moira breathed a sigh of relief that Dave had returned her call. "I need someone to talk to that I can trust and who has some grey matter between their ears. I need advice and I thought you might be able to help."

"That's fine. When do you want to meet and where? I am pretty much a free spirit over the next couple of days," Dave said.

"There's a pub just the other side of Borrowash. It's new and nobody knows me. Would that be OK? Could we meet up about seven tonight?" Moira asked.

Dave knew of the pub, The Rocket Man he thought it was called, and thought that it was a strange name for a pub with no connection to the aero engine or space industry. Perhaps it was a reference to the fireworks factory down the road, he thought. "Yes. Sure. I'll be there at seven and sitting in a window seat," he replied, hoping that neither would be recognised by someone who would tell her husband.

*

The pub was just off the main road on a housing estate. Dave had arrived early to make sure of a table near the window.

"Before you start getting the wrong idea, I'm not looking to restart our old relationship. I want some advice as an intelligent friend," Moira said as Dave placed a lime and lemonade in front of her. "It's Patrick. I'm really worried about him. He's just gone completely into himself since our Joe died, and I think he may be thinking of killing himself. I can't talk to my doctor and none of my friends would understand, and I think part of it may be down to me. I may have made a big mistake."

"Look. I'll do anything I can to help. If that means listening, I'm very good at that, but if there's anything else I can do I will. Trust me."

Moira tried to smile. It looked a bit lop-sided, and she quietly told Dave everything, from Patrick coming out of prison and how he got his job, to the initial blackmail of the Colonel, but she didn't mention the death of O'Malley. That, she thought, would stack up too many negatives against her husband. She was not going to confess on his behalf so she stuck to her story that the blackmail was only about the Colonel's liking for boys.

Dave needed time to think. There were too many loose ends. The Colonel was rising out of the mire as a more important player and he could become central to their investigations. What really interested Dave though was Moira's description of her husband's decline from near teetotal and hard working, to the classic signs of alcoholism and paranoia. Something had seriously spooked him. Perhaps Simon's thoughts about a link between father and son's death were closer than he'd first thought.

*

Simon was happy to go along to Paul Ruthin's party. It was not going to be over-stocked with girls, but what the heck, it was a night out and there was the prospect of decent conversation as well as a few beers. Paul's parties were generally the ultimate antidote to the gatherings he normally attended in flats and shared houses around the town, where the format was loud music, Party Seven gassy, canned beer, and joints of varying quality being passed round. Admittedly the joints were by far the best element.

Paul's parties were different. Being gay did not stop him inviting a broad range of guests. You could be sitting with the contenders for the Press Ball, or sharing a whisky, rum or vodka with a guy who'd just come back from Cannes or Switzerland, and, of course, there was the contingent of visiting homosexuals, including some really interesting guys. The nearest comparison to Paul's parties was one of the better nights at Mario's in Nottingham, but with more style. The whole evening was not about who you were going to sleep with, it was about freedom of expression and meeting people who didn't believe in barriers.

It was gone midnight and Simon was thinking of calling it a day – he may have just been on holiday, but he was very tired – and then there was a commotion at the door. Paul was standing in front of a well-dressed middle-aged bloke who was talking too loudly, while Paul was whispering in his ear. "Time to go," Simon said to himself and moved towards the door.

"You look like a nice young man. Who are you?" the middle-aged, obviously drunk, guy said, breaking off from talking to Paul.

Paul shrugged and moved slightly away. "Simon, meet

Colonel Hamilton-Pocklington, a friend who normally does not attend my events. Certainly not unless he's had a few too many," Paul glared at his guest.

"Simon is a reporter on the *Derby Telegraph* and a good mate, so don't go upsetting him," he added.

The Colonel did a quick double-take and a sober look flooded his face.

"Pleased to meet you. I've known Paul a long time and my friend and I thought we'd drop in for a late drink," he said, indicating a thirty-something woman alongside him. It was clear that they had both just left a dinner, with the Colonel in full dinner jacket and bow tie, and the woman in a well-cut evening gown.

"My friend was having such a pleasant evening she didn't want it to end, and we'd heard Paul was hosting a bit of a bash," the Colonel said, allowing his face to relax a little and the overdose of alcohol to show through. His ladyfriend was also clearly in the stage of drunkenness where she'd had enough, but not enough to satisfy her, and a final brandy or two would send her over the edge.

Simon was not going to let this opportunity go and he smiled at the Colonel. "I'm sure Paul will make you very welcome," he said, putting out his hand to be shaken by both the Colonel and his lady. "I'll get a couple of drinks, what would you like?"

Paul gave him a slightly exasperated look, but realised that Simon had actually let him off the hook. The Colonel and his friend looked out of place, but it was a pretty eclectic crowd tonight, and he really could not turn them away. Simon's intervention meant he could allow them in, but didn't have to entertain them with his own conversation.

"I'll get the drinks," he said. "You three grab that table

before it's taken," indicating the small table against the curved, velour bench seat and stool with matching velour cover.

Simon led the way and invited them to sit on the bench while he sat on the stool.

"You look a little grandly dressed for this place," he smiled as he spoke generally to both of them.

"We've been to a dinner at The Friary, some industry thing, and we thought we'd escape and have a last drink here. I'm Amanda, by the way, as Tim seems to have forgotten how to introduce people," the woman said, with a pleasant smile to the Colonel and a touch of his arm to show that she didn't mean any insult or reproach.

It was almost the last thing she said, as the Colonel concentrated his full attention on Simon and began asking questions about his life as a reporter and whether he had a girlfriend, fiancée or wife. Simon could read some people and this guy was crystal clear. He was making a play for him. The light touch of the Colonel's hand on his arm as he threw back his head to laugh and the knee that touched his leg under the table were the giveaways. Simon knew that, without the drinks, the Colonel would have been much more controlled and would have hidden his homosexuality, but he didn't mind the approach. Firstly, he had no prejudice against queers, that was just the way they were, and since getting into Derby's music scene he had met and was friends with loads of such guys. They were not just harmless, but great fun to be with and several showed immense talent, professionally and artistically. Secondly, the Colonel was a key figure in the investigation into Joe Mahoney's death.

Now was not the time to take this further, but the Colonel was keen to get closer to Simon. His light touches on his arm had not been rejected and Simon hadn't flinched when his knee accidentally touched his leg two or three times.

"You're involved in the firm building the new ring road aren't you?" Simon asked. "I've been getting a feature together on it and I've already spoken to Councillor Moores. Could I ask you a few questions? Not tonight, obviously, but sometime over the next day or two?"

The Colonel was not going to let the opportunity for a little tryst escape and he felt secure talking in platitudes about the ring road project. "Yes, of course. Why don't we meet up? Not tomorrow, but the next day? Unless you don't work over the weekend?"

"No. I work all day, every day. That's the nature of the job. Where shall we meet?"

The Colonel allowed himself a little smile. I'll get this youngster home as soon as I can, he thought.

"Give me a call and I'll send a car to pick you up. We can meet at Morley Manor. Do you know it?" the Colonel asked.

Simon nodded and finished his drink. He looked at his watch and stood. Apologising, he explained he had to work the next day, but looked forward to calling the Colonel. He shook hands with him and then turned to the Colonel's companion who had, by now, had the two brandies and was on the verge of falling asleep. She opened one eye, then the other and wriggled upright, sticking out a hand to Simon and forcing a smile that didn't really fit her face.

Simon called Paul over on his way out and asked him to apologise to Tom when he turned up. He then almost skipped down the stairs and out on to Babington Lane. The ten minutes it took him to walk home flew by.

At 8am he was in the office – holidays were for wimps and he could always say he had music reviews to do – and a few minutes later Dave appeared, noticed the broad smile on Simon's face and came across to his desk. Simon started to blurt out about his meeting with the Colonel, but Dave stopped him.

"Not the right time or place, and I also have some developments to report. Let's meet up at lunchtime. Can you get to Duffield? I don't want to be seen in town at the moment, and the White Hart will have nobody in who recognises us," Dave said. "12.30 be OK?"

Simon agreed. He knew of the pub, but had not been in. The Red Lion was his favourite in Duffield, especially the landlord's tall, exceptionally good-looking, vivacious daughter.

"I'll go first. I think what you hear about the Colonel will have a big impact on your meeting with him," Dave said, settling with a pint of Worthington. This was a good pub, with a discreet little area where their quiet conversation would be lost in the hubbub of the lunchtime crowd.

"Your thoughts about a possible link involving Joe, his dad and the ring road project may well have legs. The Colonel is being blackmailed by Mahoney's wife, Moira, and that, in my eyes, gives him reason enough to up the ante. So far it's not bad blackmail, if you can ever have such a concept, and the amounts involved are small, but it puts my view of Moira in a different light. Blackmailing someone because they are a homosexual is so 1950s, or even last century, at the very best and, even if what he is doing is illegal with the age of the boys involved, I'm surprised that Moira has taken such a massive step, or that the Colonel has fallen for it.

"What really interests me is the way that her husband has gone downhill in recent months. They had a fantastic Christmas, she says, but a month later he was a different person. He started going down to the Crown Club in Spondon, not just once or twice a week, but every night. Since he never used to drink more than a couple of pints, maybe four or five a week, the change has been dramatic. Something has spooked him, and it must be a lot more serious than the Allenton farm business.

"What we have got to do is find out what it was, and I'm hoping that your meeting with the Colonel will help us unlock this mystery."

Simon was quiet. His forthcoming meeting with the Colonel was looking a more difficult, if interesting, prospect.

"I'm going up to Morley Manor tomorrow. I know it's a Sunday, but I'm free and he doesn't seem to operate a normal week. A bit like us really," Simon smiled at Dave. "At the moment I'm thinking of an interview based on Derwent Bank Construction and a personal angle about him, being Derbyshire born and bred, playing such a major role in the future face of the town. It will massage his ego and, as well as a decent feature for the *Telegraph*, I might find out more of what's really going on."

Dave nodded. He was grateful for Simon's input, but he had to remember he was still a rookie reporter and the growing complexity around the death of Joe Mahoney was a potential minefield. There was no alternative. If they were to find out why and how Joe died, they needed to get more involved with the main players, and the Colonel was clearly someone who was either directly involved or knew the people who were.

"Good angle, and you're covering your back with the

newspaper nicely," he told Simon. "Once you've buttered him up – and I don't mean physically, although that's what he's probably thinking, so be bloody careful – you can ask a few more searching questions.

"He may be all bluster and bonhomie, but there are a few things working in our favour. First off, he's not fully aware that you're straight and he thinks he's got a chance. That could be a bit problematic, but I'm fairly sure you can handle him. His ego, when you invite him to talk about how important he is, will overcome his disappointment about not having you as a playmate. Secondly, he's being blackmailed and that would be disconcerting for anybody. What we really need him to do is talk about his relationships – especially Patrick Mahoney, the husband of the woman who's blackmailing him and the right-hand man he rescued when he came out of prison, even if that was also down to Moira."

Dave then explained, using his well-honed experience, the art of journalistic interviewing. It was not, he said, simply a matter of asking a question and then writing down the answer, it was much more about leading the interviewee into a state of mind where they are happy to talk about things that, at the beginning, they would rather have kept secret. If you can leave an interviewee thinking they have said all the right things, but with a slight unease about whether they have said too much, then the job has been done.

Dave had been following these ground rules for years as the crime reporter, and he knew they worked, whether he was talking to the Chief Constable or the mother of some sad, unfortunate druggie who'd died after an overdose.

# 13

---

SIMON had made the call that afternoon and the Rolls-Royce appeared outside the *Telegraph* offices at 10.35, just five minutes late, and with the Colonel behind the wheel. He'd dressed in a tight-fitting pair of jeans and a loose shirt, and looked for all the world like those pictures Simon had seen of elderly hippies in San Franscisco for whom the big floral designs were a step too far. Opening the passenger door, the Colonel smiled and patted the deep leather seat, and Simon got in.

The drive to Morley Manor passed in a string of pleasantries. Simon was not going to declare his heterosexuality until he and the Colonel were on first name terms and the Colonel had been able to demonstrate his hospitality. Turning the car around and driving him back was a lot easier than throwing him out of the house when he'd just given him coffee and biscuits, Simon thought.

The house was impressive. Not ostentatious, but a solid block of brick fronted by a large, imposing red front door with two cream columns either side. The entrance from the road was hidden by trees, and the house only became apparent after a couple of hundred yards as the drive curved round. Wrought-iron fencing separated the large oval of grass in front of the house from the field dotted with sheep. The Colonel stopped the car right outside the door and they got out.

"The help is off today so I'll have to make the coffee," the Colonel said, thinking that one day he really would have to employ someone to stay in the house and be his manservant, but they would need to be very discreet and understanding of his ways. He could not afford to have people knowing too much about him.

In a few minutes, as expected, Simon was seated on a leather settee with a milky coffee and facing a plate of chocolate biscuits. I may be an independent, professional man earning my own wage and living by myself, but this is just like being treated by mum at home, he thought.

"This is a splendid house," he said as the Colonel sat down next to him. "I suppose it's one of the benefits of coming from a land-owning family, but I'm sure it costs a lot to keep up."

The Colonel murmured his agreement and settled himself next to his young guest.

"Can I be honest with you Colonel?" Simon said, moving slightly away and putting his knees together. "I find it a bit uncomfortable being this close to a man. I'm a reporter for the local newspaper and what I would really like to do is interview you. I really admire what you are doing and the way you're leading the ring road project."

Simon carried on, desperate not to be thrown out after rejecting what appeared to be the Colonel's first advances. "You're such a well-known and well-respected member of Derbyshire society, and you could just live a life of leisure, but you have committed yourself, not just to business and creating hundreds of jobs in the town and county, but also to being a central figure in the biggest development the town has ever seen. I will understand if you ask me to leave, but I was really pleased when you invited me here. It would be great for my career if I was able to interview you for the *Telegraph*. A real feather in my cap."

The Colonel got up and walked over to the stone fireplace. He was upset, not because this young lad was turning him down – that had happened far too many times for him to worry about – but that he knew he was queer. He tried hard to hide his sexuality, and surely the fact that Amanda had come along to Paul's little soirée had disguised it? Obviously not. But this was, he thought, an opportunity to put the personal problems aside and get back on track with promoting Derwent Bank and the ring road project. It would also be one in the eye for Clive Browne.

"Young man, you are a guest in my house and will be treated as such. I hope I didn't give you the wrong impression. You are always welcome here, and of course I will be happy to talk to you about the ring road project, it will be my pleasure. However, let's get things off to the right start. I'm Tim, not Colonel, not when we are in my house." The Colonel beamed a smile at Simon and proffered the plate of biscuits, taking a seat opposite instead of next to him.

"Can you tell me a bit about your family history? I've read the library archives, but hearing it first hand would give me more of a flavour," Simon began.

The Colonel gave Simon a truncated family history. It was not something he was greatly proud of as, if truth be told and he'd rather it wasn't, his father was a wastrel and a gambler and he'd become a father late in life. In a bid to make a man of his only son, Tim had been enrolled in the Royal Army Service Corps and managed to get to Colonel rank, meaning he did not have to cook, instead spending his time in Aden advising more senior ranks on catering for the troops on the front line. It had been pure guesswork as he had no idea what they wanted, and little interest.

Morley Manor had been passed down the Pocklington family for generations, along with properties in Derbyshire, Lincolnshire and Norfolk, and in the end it was really all that was left of a once large, property-based empire, apart from a few farms. Still, no need to let those facts get in the way of a good British heritage story, he thought.

"You've headed up Derwent Bank Construction for about ten years I believe," Simon said, anxious to get the interview on to the right track. "Winning the ring road contract must have been a great achievement. What has it meant to you and the company?"

The Colonel was on safe ground here and he was able to expand on how, under his leadership and with his business contacts, Derwent Bank had risen to become a major force in the county, with over a thousand employees working on the ring road project alone.

"I shouldn't really be telling you this, but it looks very likely that the project will be extended and Derwent Bank will be responsible for extensions that will eventually lead to a whole new inner ring road, completing the circle. Our relationship with the Town Council is extremely strong and we are working closely with the Planning Department," he said.

"What about finance? The council won't be putting all the money up front will they? Are they using outside help?" Simon asked, aware that finance was normally a thorny subject when the council was asked direct, but hoping that the Colonel would be a bit more forthcoming.

"Yes. There's a developer involved in securing the day-to-day finance, but Derwent Bank is working closely and directly with the council," the Colonel said, dismissing the implied suggestion that there were other third parties.

"So where is the finance coming from? Is it someone you know? Are you personally, and as a respected Derbyshire businessman, more involved than simply the main contractor? If that's so then it makes an even better story for Derwent Bank," Simon replied, picking up on the short, sharp answer the Colonel had given previously.

"If the truth be told, I am very close to the developer, and as you have pointed out, my involvement is in the whole project, not just Derwent Bank. It's something I can feel rightly proud of. The developer is Clive Browne in Nottingham. He is rock solid and blue chip, so we have no problems in securing the finance and he will see nothing until we actually hand the completed project over to the council. At that stage he will get his money back, plus the agreed percentage, but you must realise that by then, because of interest rates and rising values, the project will be worth a lot more than the council has paid. It's difficult for the layman to understand, but you can be assured that I am securing a great deal for the town."

So, Simon thought, all the money is coming from somewhere else, and the Colonel is keen to play down the involvement of this Clive Browne. That's another name to research.

"You must feel very proud of the Derwent Bank staff, especially Patrick Mahoney. I understand he has been your right-hand man as well as the overall foreman."

Simon said, moving the interview into the area where he wanted some detailed answers.

"The Derwent Bank staff have done, and are doing, their job and working very hard. I'd rather Mahoney wasn't mentioned by name in your report, we've had a few problems recently and there is a possibility that we will have to let him go, but that's just between you and me."

"But I thought he was your main man. Has this got anything to do with the death of his son, the man who worked for the Planning Department?" Simon was getting close to the heart of the matter and he wanted the Colonel to carry on opening up. "I've been told that without Mahoney this contract wouldn't be on time or on budget."

"I don't know where you got that information from, but it's totally false. Mahoney was brought on board by me and he did a great job for a few months, but recently he has been going downhill. I need people I can trust implicitly and right now that doesn't include him. Like I said, it's best if you leave his name out completely, for everybody's sakes, including his." The Colonel was getting a bit red-faced again, so Simon just nodded and decided to change tack back to ego massage.

"Councillor Moores must be grateful for the way you're handling this project," he said. "Do you think the council will give you some sort of honour, or at least recognition, when it's all over?"

"Don't talk to me about that man." The Colonel was very red-faced now, and Simon was surprised at the response. "He and that Clive Browne like to think they are running this whole project, but they are not. It's me. Do you know what they're planning for a memorial?

They are having a plaque made to be set into one of the bridge supports with all their names on it, and Derwent Bank Construction in small letters at the bottom. It's an insult, a bloody insult."

Simon's brain was recording every comment, but he had very noticeably closed his notebook.

"Don't use any of that in your article," the Colonel said, calming down and breathing slowly.

"Of course not. I haven't taken any notes. I fully understand your disappointment, but at least you will have the knowledge that it was you that led the project. I really should be going now. You've been very helpful. I'll get one of our photographers to go out to the site. Would it be OK if they contacted you direct, and then we can get some photos of you as well?" Simon asked, noting the very positive response from the Colonel.

He declined the offer of the lift back into town. He wanted time to think about what the Colonel had been saying, and a walk to Morley village and then a bus ride into Derby would help. They shook hands and Simon was pleased to note that, instead of the limp handshake he had expected, the Colonel's was firm and friendly.

The Colonel watched the young reporter walk down the drive and then took a glass out of the cabinet, nearly filled it with Aberlour and took a deep draught. He really should not have exploded like that about Moores and Browne, but they shouldn't be pushing him out, he thought. Anyway, that bit would not be appearing anywhere because he hadn't taken any notes. And he was fairly sure that Mahoney's name would not appear in the press. It was important to keep him out of the limelight.

\*

"You," Simon said as he marched into the Exeter Arms and pointed at Dave, "owe me a pint. No, make that two!"

Dave and Tom both laughed and Dave put his hands up. "OK, I'll get the round in, but you obviously survived. I knew you could handle him. How did it go?"

Simon nodded to Tom and sat down at the table. He gave a full account of his visit to Morley Manor and then added: "What do you know about this Clive Browne guy? He's clearly some big shot if he is fronting the project's finances, but the Colonel doesn't seem to think a lot of him."

"What we have here, Simon, is a clear case of the junior business partner in a project being trodden on by a more senior one, and he's hitting out." Dave settled down to take centre stage. "The Colonel wants all the glory for himself, and he seems to think he is being pushed out by Councillor Moores as well. With the apparent cooling of his attitude towards Mahoney we now have four main players in the mystery: the Colonel, who is being lined up as a scapegoat, but we don't know why yet; Clive Browne, who is involved, but we don't know how much; and John Moores, who is obviously involved in what has happened and is linked through Joe Mahoney as well as the project. He may be the link we're looking for.

"The fourth is Joe's dad, Patrick. Tom has given us a full background. He's not averse to criminal activity, as his past shows, and he seems to have become a lush over recent weeks. My contacts in CID tell me that the uniforms are sniffing around the ring road site because they think there's something dodgy going on, plus it's known that young Joe Mahoney had been there a few times. Old man Mahoney isn't happy. He's carrying on doing his job, but seems to be spending more time at the Crown in Spondon, and is rarely sober."

Tom butted in: "Yes Dave, that's what I've heard, and it's not just Mahoney who's upset. There are quite a few guys working there with recent histories that don't bear scrutiny. They want this whole job over and done with, and the police out of the way, pronto.

"Earlier this year one of the guys noticed that there had been some odd activity before he arrived on the site for the evening shift. The crane and bucket looked as if they'd been played with – and whoever did it had gone and cleaned the bucket. That never happens. And last week someone had done the most remarkable clean-up in the site office, and that hasn't seen a cleaner since the job started.

"These guys are no fools and with their past history they can tell when something is untoward. The comments I've been getting back are that it looks as if someone has been making sure that there are no identifying marks anywhere, and that includes boot prints, jacket fibres and anything else that the forensic boys could find. It's been too clinical."

"Thanks Tom," Dave said. "Just keep in the background as much as possible will you. We're dealing with an unexplained, violent death and I don't want you compromised.

"Now that we've spoken with the Colonel and Moira that leaves three people we need to stay close to. I'll get to Mahoney – my reputation for beer drinking will stand me in good stead when I get round to meeting him. Simon, I need you to find out more about the Moores involvement. Did you manage to rearrange a meeting?"

Simon nodded. "Yes, I'll speak to him soon."

Dave seemed distracted and didn't acknowledge Simon's response. "Tom, could you dig up as much as you can about Clive Browne?

"We're getting closer. I can feel it in my water, but we need to be careful. A DJ and two newspaper reporters are small fry to career criminals, if that is what we're facing."

# 14

---

DAVE walked into the Crown Club to be greeted by his usual welcome from Mike.

"Look what the cat's dragged in. Where've you been these last few millennia?"

"Here, waiting to get served," Dave replied and warmly shook Mike's hand.

"What'll it be then? The Bass is looking good."

"Smooth talking bastard, and here's me about to go teetotal. OK you've broken my pledge. A pint will be great," Dave responded. "Would you believe I'm not here just to gaze into your eyes and whisper sweet nothings? I need to pick your brains, and I've even brought my own shovel," he added, and took a sip of the pint Mike placed in front of him. "Hmm. You're right. That is good."

Mike leaned slightly over the bar. "And how can I help my old mucker then?"

"Customer of yours: one Patrick Mahoney. I'd like to meet him if you could do the introductions."

"That miserable old sod? A year ago I hardly saw him, but since January he's become a regular fixture almost every night – early doors through to closing. He can't half put it away though, so don't be upsetting one of my best customers. He's over there by the wall. I'll introduce you."

They moved across to where Mahoney was sitting.

"Hi Patrick. Gentleman here wants a word, but he's promised not to upset you. If he does you have my permission to knock him into next week. Dave Green, local newspaper reporter, meet Patrick Mahoney, a man of discerning taste when it comes to beer and where to drink it." Mike watched as the two men shook hands and returned to his bar. Nothing to do with me, he thought. Stay on the right side of the law, the local newspaper and the customers, that's my motto and it's served me well.

Mahoney felt a shudder down his spine as he looked at Dave. Not another bloody journalist with his questions, but I can't lose my temper or walk off. Got to be as natural as possible, he thought.

"Waiting for the band?" Dave asked. "I'll get you a pint since you're nearly finished. You like the jazz then?"

"Aye. I'm a big fan of Jim Finney on the ivories. He could go places. Don't really know why he's stuck to Derby," Mahoney said as Mike brought his beer over. "What do you want to speak to me about then?"

It was the killer question. If Mahoney saw through his bluff now the whole idea was dead and buried. He hoped that his friendly face, plus the beers that Mahoney had already had, would make it a bit easier.

"It's the drummer, Alan Morton," he said. "He's seen you here just about every time he's played and because I'm a reporter with a bit of an interest in jazz he suggested I have a word with you. It's not important. If you don't want to say anything that's OK."

Mahoney nodded. "Yeah. I like the jazz down here. What does he want to know? Why doesn't he ask me himself?"

"Alan's an editor; it's my job as a reporter to put the words on paper. He looks at them later, and anyway, he says he's a bit too close to the music to be writing about it."

Mahoney nodded again and started to talk about his love of jazz, a love that had grown since he'd become a regular at the Crown. Once he started talking he relaxed and gradually became more animated as he reminisced about the recent visits of out-of-town musicians, including his personal favourite, Kathy Stobart.

Half an hour disappeared quickly and the Jim Finney Quintet started a slow-paced set to gradually warm up the fairly sparse crowd. Dave said nothing and, out of the corner of his eye, watched as Mahoney's whole being, body and soul, relaxed: a combination of several pints and good music.

Mahoney went to the bar and brought back two more pints, one for him and the other for Dave. As he sat down a card fell from his wallet, with his photograph on. It was the Derwent Bank Construction security card.

"Oh, I see you work on the new ring road. Is everything going to plan?" Dave asked, passing the card back to Mahoney.

"I'm not really that bothered at the moment. I lost my son, so I've taken some time off work," Mahoney mumbled into his beer.

"Oh, I'm so sorry. I should have realised. You're, the father of that lad who died. It must be dreadful. Are they treating you OK? They've given you time off anyway."

"My boss is an ignorant idiot. I used to see him as a mate – a very wealthy one and a million miles apart from me as a person – but he was a genuine guy. He paid well, gave me responsibility and backed me up when I made decisions on site," Mahoney said.

"Now, not only is he always taking holidays, but when he is there the council keep coming on site to see what's happening. Even my lad Joe was given the job of making sure I was doing my job, and now his boss, Councillor Moores, keeps wandering over from his big office in the Council House."

So, no love lost between Mahoney and both the Colonel and John Moores, Dave thought.

"Your lad must have been good for Moores to trust him with supervising the project for the council," Dave said.

"Best lad I ever had or could ever hope for." Mahoney was beginning to let the beer do the talking. "He could've gone to college or university and got a degree or something, but no, he wanted a job with a career and prospects, and where's it got him? Markeaton Crematorium. It should have been me. My life's finished, his was just beginning."

Dave let the conversation die. Finished his pint and got two more. As he returned to the table and put the fresh one in front of Mahoney he said: "I've heard tell they run a tight ship at the ring road site. One of the guys who's been there recently was remarking on how clean the site office is – no muddy boot prints and every surface so clean you could eat your dinner off it. If that's down to you it sounds like you're a lot better than Derwent Bank deserves."

Mahoney's head lifted up and he glared at Dave. "Who told you that? Who's been on site without permission? Is it the police? What were they doing in the office? Why are you asking me all these questions? I've had enough of this conversation and all your prying. Go somewhere else when you want to be a reporter. I've had enough," Mahoney took his now half full pint, finished it at the bar and then walked out.

"Thanks a bundle. He'd better come back or my takings will go down," said Mike as he dried a glass and then smiled. "Don't worry, he'll be back. It'll take more than a few questions from the ace reporter to put him off his nightly walk," he added, taking any heat or venom out of his first comment.

"Thanks Mike," Dave said. "I didn't mean to upset him, but it has been a very useful meeting. I owe you one. Dinner at the Taj sometime?"

The Wagon and Horses was getting a small boost in takings as a result of Dave Green's investigations. He, Simon and Tom met again the next evening to share their recently acquired knowledge. Dave filled them in on the Mahoney meeting, and both Tom and Simon nodded as the facts began to blend with what they had picked up.

"From where I sit, it looks like the Colonel is becoming the linchpin, the fulcrum around which several aspects are balanced," he finished.

Tom took over with an account of what he had picked up about Clive Browne. It was a straightforward history of the man, or what was known about him, but he grabbed their attention as he spoke about the enforcers on Browne's payroll.

"These guys are well known to the police, especially Marcus and Shaun. They have a reputation as animals with no human feelings, just a blind devotion to do whatever Browne says.

"The police in Nottingham have been trying to catch Browne out for years, but he always seems to stay out of trouble. There have been several civil engineering and construction projects over the years where he's provided the finance, without, it seems, borrowing from the banks, and then making a massive twenty or thirty per cent profit. He's got his nose in almost every development in the East Midlands, but he seems to keep it just clean.

"The word from the Nottingham and Derbyshire mafia – well, they're not mafia, just people in the know – is that Colonel Hamilton-Pocklington is in Browne's pocket over the Derby ring road project. Derwent Bank will get a percentage for the construction work, but they'll be paying a big chunk to Browne as commission, and Browne has also taken charge of the suppliers and service providers. Nothing can be proved, and that's going to frustrate my friends in CID horribly.

"The other element, and I'm sure Simon will have picked up on this, is that Browne has been getting very cosy with Moores in the Planning Department in recent months."

Simon had followed up his postponed interview with Moores by phoning Mavis and squeezing himself into a busy schedule. The bluster of the first short meeting had been followed with slightly more bluster during the half-hour time-slot that Moores had granted him.

It hadn't been difficult to find out that, in his opinion, Moores knew very little. The only interesting snippet was the extremely high regard in which he held Clive Browne, in almost complete contrast to the way he dismissed the Colonel as head of Derwent Bank.

"I've got enough for a short feature article, but it will be difficult to cut out the platitudes and waffle if I quote him verbatim," Simon said.

"My gut feeling is that Moores is not involved. I'm not saying he's incorruptible, but I do think he is incapable of the devious mind needed to tell lies and keep up a pretence. I just don't think he's that smart. Plus, I am now convinced, having spoken to him direct, that he wasn't involved in any way in the death of Joe Mahoney. Put simply, I don't think he's clever enough."

"You've done great work there Simon, and I'm fully prepared to accept your judgment on Moores. Do you agree Tom?" Dave turned to his friend who nodded in agreement.

"So that leaves three. Browne is covered in smooth and slick – nothing is going to stick to him – so we are left with Hamilton-Pocklington and Mahoney. I'm going to have another chat with Mahoney. I know he's hiding something."

"I'll come with you if you like, and if it's going to be at the Crown Club Alan has asked me to cover a gig there by some guy called Robin Skidmore," Simon said.

"OK, but I don't want to spook Mahoney by having more of us than is necessary. He's a big bloke and even with a few pints inside him he could flatten me. Let's meet down there, but be independent of each other," Dave said and turned to Tom.

"I hate to say this, but I think we may be getting a bit too close to the end result for comfort. If we do find out what happened to young Joe, then whoever was responsible will not take kindly to our sniffing around. What are the chances you could discreetly alert some of your old mates in CID?"

"Discretion and the police are not normally words I'd use together," Tom said smiling. "If I give them the teeniest little hint they'll put it in a book, forget about it, and then ask me to confess to as many unsolved petty crimes as they can find to get their arrest rate up.

"So far the police have succeeded in making life difficult for everybody on the ring road site, and got John Moores and his lovely PA scrabbling to cover up any favours he might have received in the course of awarding contracts. I think we should stick together and be your back-up. You'll be going by bus, I presume, unless Simon can use one of the office cars, and I'll have my mighty motor, so we can be fairly mobile if required."

Clive Browne was concerned. His contacts in Derby had kept him up to date with the police activity at the site, and he knew that nothing could link him and his business with the death of young Mahoney, but having Marcus and Shaun around was problematic. Thankfully they knew it too. Injury, like a bit of bruising and a few broken bones, to dissuade people from continuing along a certain track or, at worst, removing them from a place or position was OK, but killing someone was a different matter.

Browne had calmed them down the day after young Mahoney's body had been dealt with and his father given the ultimatum, but they were no use to him now. They firmly believed that they would be judged murderers – a view Browne was not going to dissuade them of, even if it was accidental death – and they were very happy when Browne gave them a car, two tickets for a ferry to France, and enough cash to keep driving until they arrived back in Karelia.

John Moores would be no problem. He was, basically, an honest man – easily manipulated but honest – and the police would find nothing untoward in his arm's length business relationship.

Tim Hamilton-Pocklington was a different matter. He had been a loose cannon for a while now. He always did what he was told, but if you weren't there to tell him he seemed at a loss as to what to do. It was getting close to the time when he would decide, with a few nudges and pushes, to resign from Derwent Bank and move to Bali permanently, and the sooner the better.

# 15

DAVE got a lift with Simon so he didn't need to get the bus, and it helped that Simon had decided he'd rather cut out the booze for an evening. Not only would he feel better being sober if Dave needed back-up, but it was always good to have a clear head when listening to the intricacies of jazz. They arrived at 8pm, with Simon going backstage to speak with Jim Finney and Dave heading for the bar.

"I hope we're not going to have a re-run of the other night," Mike said as he poured Dave's pint.

"No, I'm here to apologise, so get Patrick a pint as well will you. Apart from his unpleasantness just at the end of the evening we seemed to get on well and I think he really, deep down, wants to unburden himself," Dave said.

Mahoney, meanwhile, had noticed Dave and Simon come in together. Two bloody reporters, he thought, recognising Simon from a previous visit when he had some girl with him. He'd calmed down after the last meeting with Dave Green. Perhaps all that prying about the clean state of the site office had just been following up on what the police were doing, and anyway, that was nothing to do with him. All he was worried about was his now dead son, and talking to Green had seemed to help.

"Don't walk out on me, or worse, I've come to

apologise. I seemed to hit a raw nerve the last time we had a drink together, and I'm really sorry about that. It must have been bad enough coming to terms with the tragic death of Joe, without some dumb reporter asking questions." Dave put the pint in front of Mahoney and sat down.

"Yeah. Well, I was a bit hasty," Mahoney said, feeling his face stretching into a tight smile – the first time for many months. "Cheers."

"It's Robin Skidmore tonight isn't it?" Dave asked, having been told so by Simon on the drive to Spondon.

"Yes. It should be good. He played tenor sax with Humphrey Lyttelton's band a long time ago and he sometimes plays with Kathy Stobart, and she's wonderful. Should be a good night," Mahoney explained. "I see you came in with that young reporter. Is he covering the session or you?"

"Oh, not me. I don't know enough about music to write about it. How come you know Simon?" Dave asked, with a warning bell ringing loudly in his head.

"Met him months ago, just before Christmas. He was in here with a girl," Mahoney said, thinking back to a time when life was very simple, he hadn't killed anybody, his son was still alive and his wife was not beset with trying to keep herself and him mentally together.

"Should be a good night," Dave said non-committally, repeating Mahoney's words and hoping that it would be a good night both musically and in getting some answers. The two settled back and enjoyed a first set that began with some traditional swing and then moved on to more adventurous sounds. There was a hint of John Coltrane, but that was probably down to Robin Skidmore's prowess on the sax and the mixture of traditional jazz with some more modern bass and piano backing. The pints flowed again, and Mahoney was surprised at how much he was enjoying the evening.

At the final encore, Simon approached Dave and Mahoney. Shaking hands with Mahoney, he said: "I'm sure we've met before, but my memory for faces is awful, especially after a couple of pints."

"Patrick Mahoney. You and some girl came and sat with me around Christmas time," he replied.

Simon banged his forehead with his palm. "I remember. That was Melanie. Haven't seen her this year," he said. "Anyway, I've got to do a couple of interviews, and the lads backstage will be hanging around for a while. Mike has already agreed to reopen the bar after the punters have gone, so if you'd still like a lift home, you'll have to hang around, Dave."

Dave had been planning to walk back with Mahoney to see if he could find out more of what happened to his son, but this was an even better opportunity.

"Yes. That's fine with me. You OK for a late drink Patrick?" he asked and Mahoney nodded and smiled.

"Look, I'm really sorry about your lad Joe. Have they got any further in finding out what happened?" Dave asked, hoping Mahoney wouldn't walk out and would, as he'd intimated, stay for a late drink or two.

"No not really. It seems that it was just an accident," Mahoney said.

"I'm sure you already know, but they're saying Joe didn't die in that alley. The police are looking into where he could have died and why his body was found there. It's quite a mystery," Dave said, and watched Mahoney as he seemed to squirm in his seat.

"In fact I'm told they're linking Joe's death to the ring

road site and the site office. I don't know why, but that's what the police are thinking. I'm just a simple reporter." Dave was watching Mahoney closely and a shadow seemed to fall across his face as his expression darkened.

"The police know nothing. Joe's death was an accident. They can ask me all they like. I didn't kill him. I had nothing to do with his death. They should be asking those two goons who killed him and attacked me." Mahoney blurted out the words before he realised what he'd said. The silence that followed was palpable. Strangely, instead of fear or anger, Mahoney suddenly felt better, as if a weight had lifted and his head was lighter.

Dave stared open-mouthed and then shook his head slightly to clear his thoughts and work out what to say next.

"Look. I'm not accusing you, but if you think it will help then you can tell me. Get it off your chest. I'm not the police, I'm not a goon. Just treat me as a sounding board and talk about it," Dave said leaning forward, as Mahoney slowly and quietly told him the full story of Joe's death.

As the final few words left his lips, and he described how his son's body had fallen to the ground in the alley, Mahoney began to shake and thought he was going to be sick. He wiped his eyes with his sleeve. He'd lost track of time, and when he looked round the club seemed almost empty. He stood up and said to Dave, "I'm going for a piss. I'll be back in a minute."

Mahoney knew he was in trouble. As he stood in the cubicle, his head resting on the wall while he directed the stream of piss into the bowl, he tried to get his thoughts together.

Dave Green was not a lifelong mate. He seemed OK

and he felt better after telling him the whole story, but he knew he needed help. The only one who could provide that help was the man who, he felt, was ultimately responsible. As he walked out of the gents he stopped at the phone and dialled Morley Manor.

The Colonel was awake, but after half a bottle of wine and a couple of very large single malt whiskies, was not as sharp as he wanted to be when he picked up the phone and realised it was Mahoney.

"We have a problem. There's a newspaper reporter here and he knows all about my son and what happened, and where. You'd better get down here now and help me out or I'll tell him all about you," Mahoney slurred down the phone.

"Where are you? What have you told him?" the Colonel asked.

"I'm at the Crown Club in Spondon, just get down here in ten minutes and I'll be in the car park waiting," Mahoney said, putting the phone down and then walking back to the table at which Dave was still sitting.

"I need some fresh air. I'm going to finish this pint and then go for a walk. You can join me if you want and I'll tell you some more about what's been going on at that ring road project," Mahoney said as he sat down and took a swig of the pint Dave had just bought for him.

Dave glanced around the club and saw that Simon was not around – still interviewing the musicians, he assumed – and Mike was in a back room somewhere. He hoped that one or the other would appear and see him walk out with Mahoney, but this was too good an opportunity to miss. All he was concerned about was

Mahoney's mental state. He was slurring his words, which was understandable considering the number of pints they'd drunk, and Mahoney had had at least three more than him, but he seemed quite calm and deliberate in his movements. There was no shaking and he had a fixed, firm, set face. Not like any drunk he'd ever seen.

"Come on. Let's get some fresh air," Mahoney said as he stood up, grabbed his jacket from the back of his chair, leaving about a quarter of a pint in his glass.

Dave did the same, but managed to finish his pint while looking round to see if Simon or Mike, the only people who knew him in the bar, had reappeared. They hadn't.

He followed Mahoney out into the car park, just as a Rolls-Royce pulled up. Mahoney opened the driver's door, pulled the Colonel out and left him lying on the broken tarmac of the car park. He got hold of Dave by the arm in a powerful grip and opened the rear door with the other hand, pushing him in.

"I'll drive. You get in the back and keep this guy company. Make sure he doesn't try anything, like getting out," Mahoney said as he picked the Colonel up and shoved him into the back and got into the driver's seat, flicking the switch to set the child locks on the rear doors. He suddenly felt sober and every action was an immediate reaction to the plan that was going round his head.

The smooth, ocean-liner-like Rolls-Royce became two tons of rabid, smoking metal as Mahoney slammed it into first and roared off the car park, spraying fragments of tarmac against the side of the club and clipping the stone pillar as he entered the road.

Simon Jardine came out of the backstage area, looked around the club room and saw neither Dave nor Mahoney. He ran through the two sets of doors and into the car park just in time to see the tail lights disappearing. As he started running towards the road he noticed another car to his right, and it pulled up alongside him: a well-cared-for Cortina with an anxious-looking Tom behind the wheel.

"Jump in, I'll try and follow them, but they've got a head start and Mahoney is throwing the Roller around like a sports car," Tom said.

Dave and the Colonel had been thrown from one side of the car to the other as it left the car park. Neither could do anything except be bounced around like dummies.

"This guy knows everything except the fact that you and I are killers. I can't go on any more telling lies and hiding the truth. Tell him about O'Malley!" Mahoney shouted at the Colonel.

"Don't be stupid, you stupid idiot! If that gets out it will ruin everything. I'll lose everything. I couldn't survive prison. Those old lags would have a field day with me. It'd be worse than if I was a copper," the Colonel pleaded. "Just slow down. Think about what you're doing. We can work this out. Nobody is going to miss a newspaper reporter and you can hole up in one of the outbuildings at the Manor."

"I said tell him! There is no way I'm going to live on the same earth as you. You may be rich, you may own a flash motor, but you're still scum, and murdering scum to boot," Mahoney was topping 100mph as he headed down the A52 past his house and swerving violently from the gravel in the gutter across the white line on the road towards the town.

"You killed him. I just wanted to stop him ripping us off. You put him in the bridge. You drowned his van at the farm!" the Colonel screamed.

"And who was telling me what to do? Who told me that everything would be OK? You're the clever bastard who had everything worked out. You're the guy who told me that nobody would notice O'Malley didn't exist any more. And what about my wonderful lad Joe? Did you arrange for him to be killed as well? Did you find the foreign goons who killed him, who beat me up and trussed me up? Who was it who was threatening me and made me drop Joe off Boots' roof?" Mahoney was shouting louder, twisting the wheel from side to side to emphasise his shouts, then he swung the car into the Pentagon Island building site.

"That wasn't me. It must have been Browne and his men. I had nothing to do with that. I'm an innocent man!" the Colonel yelled.

It was the last thing he ever said as Mahoney turned round and grabbed him. The car went out of control and a wing scraped a concrete pillar – possibly the one that was O'Malley's grave. Mahoney kept his foot slammed down on the accelerator. The car hit an inclined plank and the vehicle rose into the air, the force of speed pushing it over the bank of the River Derwent into mid-air, then it hit the surface of the water with a loud splash. It quickly began to sink beneath the fast-flowing water.

Tom in his Cortina had not been able to catch up, but he knew that Mahoney would not leave the main road. That Rolls-Royce was not built for swinging fast round corners, and he was no James Bond. As they approached the Pentagon Island Simon saw two red lights in the distance, pointed and shouted to Tom, and then the lights went out and it was just black where they had been.

Tom wasn't going to get his car stuck in the mud and debris of a building site so he pulled over and ran towards where the lights had been. In the spotlights of the building site on this side of the river and those from the Council House windows on the other, they saw the top of the Rolls-Royce as it sank beneath the water.

"Dave!" Simon screamed and ran to the bank.

"There! On the other side," Tom shouted back and pointed to a bedraggled figure struggling to clamber up a muddy bank. "Hold on Dave. We'll be with you," he shouted again.

Tom and Simon ran back to the car, and Tom roared off the site, getting the maximum torque out of the engine, much more than he'd ever done before. They headed out on to the old road near the Exeter Arms, over the bridge and into the Council House gardens. There they found Dave sitting up, covered in mud, soaked and shivering. Tom wrapped him in a travel blanket and together they almost carried him to the car.

"How did you get out?" Simon asked.

Dave smiled weakly. "They were too interested in grappling with each other to worry about me. I'd tried the door, but it was locked from the inside, so I wound down the window, and as we hit the water I took a deep breath and swam out. I don't think we'll see those two again."

Blue lights appeared behind them and two police constables came round to the driver's door of Tom's

Cortina. Dave's attitude was resigned, almost as if he was waiting for the stereotypical "What's going on here then?" when one of the policemen asked: "Are you OK? Did you fall in?"

Two hours later, sitting either side of Dave's bed at the Royal Infirmary, Simon and Tom listened to his story, as did DI Ludden, who'd been called out just as he was about to slide into his bed.

"You're a bunch of bloody amateurs. Why didn't you tell us sooner?" he asked Dave.

"Because I had no facts to back anything up, that's why. I was, like a good journalist, just trying to get a story. If I'd told you, the response would have been zilch. Without facts you can't move; as a reporter, I work on a hunch and then get the facts to back it up."

# 16

---

Dave was sitting opposite Moira at her house. Mary and Patrick had gone out for a walk after their mother had promised she would be all right and explained that Dave was a family friend.

"I'll always miss Patrick. Deep down he was a good man, but, and I know this sounds daft, all this horrible business has brought us really close as a family. Patrick and Mary have been incredibly good. They've both taken holiday time and they've never left me alone for a minute. Mary has even taken to coming to sit with me when I eventually go to bed. David and Martin are changed boys. They were going off the rails a little bit, and I suppose when they had had no real father for so many years that was to be expected, but now they really are grown men," Moira was explaining.

"I thought the worst bit was going to be having my blackmail aired in public and ending up in court, but Agnes, the Colonel's sister, came to see me and explained that while she was going to have to close the account that was giving me £200 a month, she would make an ex-gratia payment of £3,000 cash for whatever services I was providing the Colonel with. She never asked, just wanted to pay me, and she's told me that I won't be accused of anything. She's a really nice lady, poles apart from her brother, and a lot cleverer.

"She's also sorting out the trust that owns Morley

Manor, and although she could move in with her family, she thinks the place has too many bad memories, so she's going to open it as a care home for the elderly. She'll still have the grounds and she'll use them to graze sheep and exercise her horses. She says that a little bit of real life and beautiful animals will help the residents of the care home and give them more to see and think about than simply getting old."

Dave had set up the meeting so that he could go over in more personal detail the story of Mahoney's last few hours. The one thing he wanted to get across was that during that last meeting in the Crown Club, Patrick Mahoney had seemed to suddenly change from a man being eaten from the inside with worry and anger, to an open guy who wanted to bare his soul. It had, he said, been a cry for help.

"I think he knew he wasn't going to survive all this. I think he made the decision while he was talking to me and telling me about the death of Joe, that he would not need to go back to prison. He wanted to be at peace, but he also wanted justice."

Dave and Moira embraced and Dave kissed her cheek.

"We'll always be friends. If there is anything I can help with, maybe just as a shoulder to cry on, call me. Are you OK for money?"

Moira smiled and held Dave's hands, arms outstretched and palms facing each other. "Yes, every-thing is fine. Agnes has already put the £3,000 in my account, and it seems that, as well as a whip-round on the construction site, Derwent Bank have doubled the pension Patrick would have got and topped it up by £10 a week, so I'm a lot better off."

DI Ludden was still smarting from the fact that he had had to get the story from Dave, rather than working it out himself, but he was being quite laid back, especially after a couple of pints in the back room of the Dolphin with the *Telegraph*'s famed crime reporter and his music-loving deputy.

"I suppose I should thank you two," he said. "We were in a bit of a quandary after the post mortem showing that Joe died elsewhere. I didn't link his death with the ring road project, and that was the one connection that was needed to solve the puzzle."

Dave nudged Simon. "I think you've got this young man to thank for that. For some reason he saw the father and son relationship as being a bit more than just that."

"That may be so, but it's still no reason for you to go off and try and get killed," DI Ludden said, determined to reinforce his position and let the two reporters know that they were just amateurs, and to let the professionals do their job.

"What's happening about O'Malley?" Dave asked.

"We've found some distant relatives in Ireland and they're coming over next week. It seems that they think it quite appropriate that he should be buried in a concrete bridge support, so they're arranging for a Catholic priest to hold a short service and at some future date they will see if they can put a little plaque up. I don't think the last bit will happen, but I'm quite happy that we don't have to order the demolition of the new bridge just to find a dead body," the DI explained, adding that they had found the drowned Land Rover along with loads of paint in a pond at a farm in Allenton that had been owned by Hamilton-Pocklington.

"There's still one loose end," Simon interjected. "What about Clive Browne and the way that Joe was killed?"

"Unfortunately, everything Dave heard in the back of that Rolls-Royce is just hearsay and if any allegations were made they would need to be backed up with rock solid facts. We don't have the evidence and I don't see a way of getting sufficient proof," the DI said.

"We've checked up on this lock-up in Shardlow by the canal and it's completely empty. Nothing at all, almost forensically cleaned. It was rented for a year, cash up front, by a guy called Kovalainen and there is no trace of him anywhere. Nothing links back to Clive Browne.

"We've also questioned Mr Browne at his office in Nottingham and he has been completely open with us. He has even given us complete free rein in his office files. There is nothing, absolutely nothing, that would give us a connection between him and any of the comments and stories you two have heard. His secretary, Sandra, is one of those types who notes everything and files it away – that's clear from her immaculate filing system – but there is no mention of clandestine meetings.

"Personally, I think it's too clean. The man is a businessman, not a bloody saint. He's hiding stuff, but we have neither the time nor the personnel, and certainly not the inclination to keep digging."

"Good story Dave. Has young Simon Jardine been helping you? Is he any use?" The editor had called Dave in to show him the day's front page lead. It was the accidental death of two people heavily involved in the ring road project, one of them the Managing Director of Derwent Bank Construction.

"Yes, Mr MacMillan, Simon's been fine and very helpful, and thank you for the day's lead."

"Well he can stay with you, but I'm still a bit worried about the amount of time he's spending on pop music. He'll never get anywhere in this job if he just sticks to one thing. You've got to get a fully rounded view." Dave smiled inwardly as he wondered if being a crime reporter involved more than crime and whether he should take on reporting Women's Institutes and council meetings as well, for a "fully rounded view".

Simon was, yet again, knackered. He was now starting another week of Crown Court. It was a fraud trial and they were the worst possible: you couldn't afford to let your concentration slip for a second, and that meant no forty winks in the press box.

What was even worse was that tomorrow he was going out to Hatton to see a band headed up by a technical university graduate whose father was also the chairman of one of Derby's most successful and highest-profile engineering companies. He just hoped the band weren't crap.

Lightning Source UK Ltd.
Milton Keynes UK
UKOW02f0933190515

251836UK00001B/4/P